CAUGHT LOOKING

A Rooster Franklin
Mystery

Caught

RANDY RUSSELL

Looking

A PERFECT CRIME BOOK

DOUBLEDAY

New York London Toronto Sydney Auckland

A PERFECT CRIME BOOK
PUBLISHED BY DOUBLEDAY
a division of Bantam Doubleday Dell Publishing Group, Inc.
666 Fifth Avenue, New York, New York 10103

DOUBLEDAY is a trademark of Doubleday,
a division of Bantam Doubleday Dell
Publishing Group, Inc.

Library of Congress Cataloging-in-Publication Data

Russell, Randy.
Caught looking: a Rooster Franklin mystery/by Randy Russell.
   p. cm.
"A Perfect Crime book."
I. Title.
PS3568.U7695C38   1992
813'.54—dc20   91-17768
CIP

ISBN 0-385-42124-9
Copyright © 1992 by Randy Russell
All Rights Reserved
Printed in the United States of America
January 1992
First Edition

10 9 8 7 6 5 4 3 2 1

With special thanks to Marlene Connor, Buster Sharbel, and G. Gregory Tobin.

CAUGHT LOOKING

Kansas City . . . Last Season

This year it had been Del Mar. Previously, Alton Benjamin Franklin had attended the Saratoga meet in August. He should have this time. The horses at Del Mar ate his lunch; the seagulls ate theirs. In fact, the only fun he had was watching the sea birds eat chicken bones, which seemed to be everywhere. They managed it in a single slide down their feathered throats. So much for the California urge, he thought, and hit the highway home, his favored East Coast and Southern tracks.

You can see Royals Stadium from the interstate. Alton's van fell into the far right lane on a whim and he found himself paying four bucks to park. He bought tickets to two good seats because the scalper wouldn't sell him one. There's no better rest stop than major league baseball.

The extra seat came in handy for his nachos tray and empty beer cups. Giant swarms of gnats clouded the lights at the stadium. With the humidity near one hundred percent, the air itself smelled like the Missouri River. When the right-field fountains came on between innings there was a smattering of damp applause from shirtless fans. Water antics were about the only thing the crowd had to cheer. The A's had the Royals shut out and everyone seemed ready to call it a night. You couldn't have started the wave with an earthquake.

After more than twenty hours on the road, Alton damn near fell asleep. Fourteen games back in late August, the Royals were out of it. So was Billy Lee Burke. He'd walked the last two batters, putting runners on first and second with no outs. The Royals were already down six runs and the heart of Oakland's league-dominating batting order was coming to the plate.

Some left-hander, whose number Alton didn't recognize, warmed up in the bull pen. Royals manager John Wathan and catcher Mike Macfarlane met at the mound. George Brett ambled over from first base. Bo Jackson picked up something off the turf in left field. Billy Lee handed Wathan the ball. Six earned runs in seven innings wouldn't help Billy Lee Burke's ERA. But it wouldn't hurt it much either.

Alton checked the scoreboard. The Royals had called up a rookie. Randall Monroe's stats were all eggs, including innings pitched in the major leagues. But he had a 1.73 ERA with the Royals' triple-A team in Omaha.

"Wouldn't want to be in his shoes," a man behind Alton said to whoever was listening. Alton bet otherwise.

All the players but the new pitcher looked short from Alton's seat, dwarfed by the lights, the humidity and their lackluster performance. Monroe stood tall on the mound. He wore something you don't usually see on major leaguers. Eyeglasses. They reflected the lights. Glasses as thick as the proverbial Coke bottle.

Hard stuff, Alton thought. The big rookies always throw hard stuff. The question, though, seemed to be where this big rookie would throw the ball, not how fast.

The left-hander walked around the mound now with his head ducked. He couldn't find the rosin bag.

"That guy can't see shit!" Another fan heard from.

But he did locate the rosin bag. Then the young hurler waved off his warm-up pitches. He was ready. Jose Canseco left the on-deck circle and took position at the plate.

"He must be loose." The conversation continued behind Alton.

"Looks more like he's lost."

Monroe leaned in from the mound to pick up the catcher's signal. Then stuck there. He seemed to be frozen in place, his neck outstretched.

"He can't see the sign," the fan groaned.

"Hell, he can't even see the plate. They probably have to blow a whistle to get him pointed in the right direction."

Finally Monroe stood erect. He dropped his glove to the mound and removed his glasses. He painstakingly polished the lenses with his shirtfront. Canseco stepped out of the box.

In the dugout, Wathan uncrossed his folded arms to move the outfield back. Bo Jackson was almost to the wall, leaning forward, pounding his glove. With any luck, Bo would get a chance to throw somebody out at third, maybe home.

Steve Palmero, the home-plate umpire, held up two closed fists, signaling no outs, and shouted, "Play ball!"

But Monroe, his glasses back in place, couldn't find the rosin bag again. He walked entirely around the mound, his head down, completing a full circle before picking it up. He stared at his feet then, to make certain he placed the left one on the edge of the rubber. Your first pitch in the majors has to be a good one.

With the crowd busy ordering beers, Monroe brought the ball up in his left hand, next to his glove. Then stepped back sideways into his stretch.

The batter stepped out of the box, confused. A pitcher is supposed to hide the ball inside the glove until the last possible moment. Canseco was uneasy with the screwup, even though it was greatly in the batter's favor. By not hiding the ball, a batter could easily eye the grip, perhaps determine the pitch, could hone in on the ball at a much earlier stage in the throw and enhance the timing of his swing.

Monroe began his head-down search for the rosin bag all over again.

"I don't believe it!" a fan said.

"They should tie a string on the rosin bag and the other end on his belt."

"Screw that. They ought to run a rope from the mound to home plate."

"He loses that thing again, I'm going out and pick it up for him."

Canseco came set. Monroe left the ball outside his glove, fingers across the red stitches, and wound himself into a full stretch. He hurled a mean fastball, his first pitch in the Show, three feet over the umpire's head. It slammed into the screen with the force of a cannon shot.

A howitzer. Alton bet the ball was as close to a hundred miles an hour as anything he'd ever seen thrown.

The crowd jeered. There were the usual catcalls. Macfarlane scrambled madly behind home plate for the white pill, coming up with it in time to hold the runners now at second and third. Officially, it was a wild pitch. Palmero tossed a new one to the pitcher's mound.

Monroe seemed to grope for the toss with his glove, as if the humidity held it up, as if he couldn't see the damn thing at all. He finally brought his glove under the ball by taking a clumsy step forward, losing his balance on the slope of the mound.

Monroe studied the rubber before carefully placing his left foot there to hold it in place. This time he gripped the ball inside his glove. His elbows in, he leaned toward home plate, squinting.

From the stretch, the rookie took a little something off the pitch and placed it high, inside. Too high, too far inside, precisely where Canseco's head had been before he bailed out backward, losing his helmet and his footing to remove himself from harm's way.

Macfarlane, ready for anything, sprang to his feet in time to catch the ball. It numbed his palm.

The crowd wouldn't shut up.

Wathan signaled Macfarlane, picked up the phone to have Montgomery get warmed. The rest of the Royals bull pen was standing, hands on the wire gate, watching for the next pitch. Alton sat up, leaned forward with anticipation. He never bet on baseball, but he could have cleaned up given odds on Monroe's next throw.

Brett joined Macfarlane, who walked the ball back to the mound. Three different coaches flashed signs to the field. The base runners relaxed. Canseco dusted himself. Another pitch like that would clear the benches. When Macfarlane returned to his place behind the plate, he stood with his mitt held out. Wathan had called an intentional walk.

The minor leaguer on the mound shook off the sign.

Macfarlane stepped sideways from the plate.

And again Monroe, straining forward and squinting, shook it off.

"Will you look at that!" a fan said with disgust. "He thinks he can pitch."

"Hope he likes the food in Omaha," another answered.

"Nebraska or Japan?"

Someone laughed.

"Wherever it is they eat raw fish and everyone chokes up on the bat."

There was another signal from the dugout. Macfarlane crouched behind the plate and put down the sign for a fastball. Montgomery would throw the fourth pitch if Monroe messed up another one.

Monroe wiped sweat from his forehead with the back of his gloved hand, knocking his cap askance and leaving it like that. This time he hadn't gone to the rosin. This time he placed his left foot firmly on the rubber. This time the tall left-hander hid the ball deep inside his glove. This time he had the batter right where he wanted him and this time he threw a ninety-three-mile-an-hour fastball right down the pipe.

It looked like an aspirin spiraling into the center of Macfarlane's mitt.

Then he threw another one, moving it inside.

The third one caught the low outside corner, caught Canseco looking.

"Strike three!" Palmero called at the top of his voice. "Yur-ur out!"

Six pitches later the side was retired.

Alton watched the local coverage of the game in a motel room a short distance down the interstate. In the clubhouse, a reporter in a blue blazer asked Randall Monroe if he'd meant to knock down the batter with his second pitch. Monroe peered at the reporter through his thick lenses. "I didn't even see him standing there," he said. Then he asked if anyone had seen a locker with his name on it.

Louisville . . . The Rainy Season

Carolyn Sakwoski wasn't happy with the rain. She wasn't happy with her life. It had poured all day, then stopped for a few hours. Now that it was Friday night the thunder started up again. It had rained three weekends in a row and Carolyn didn't know what she was doing stuck in this blue-collar mudhole named Louisville.

After Paul had been killed, she'd wanted to move somewhere nice. Kentucky had sounded right; but it wasn't. As displeased with her life as with the weather, Carolyn ferociously chomped cold pizza from the fridge. Sadness, anger, an overall regret kept her from going to bed after a hot bath. Carolyn couldn't put her finger on it.

Dammit, she thought, *it's everything.*

She and Sarah had spent the day sorting returns at Carolyn's bookstore. She held onto a few titles that they both knew would likely never sell. Carolyn hated returning unsold books to the publishers. Unread books were lonely girls waiting to be asked to the dance.

She'd turned forty-one in April. What was *she* waiting to be asked to?

When her sister called with a family crisis, Carolyn was pleased to be asked to help. She hadn't seen her little sister in years. An age difference of thirteen years had kept them from being close. On top of which, Marilyn was a blonde. And had grown up like one, a cheerleader in street clothes.

"You called the right place, sis," Carolyn insisted. "I know just the person and he owes me a favor. Make that a hundred favors."

"I don't know what anyone can do. I just needed someone to talk to. He's gone crazy. Absolutely crazy. I was thinking of leaving the house."

"Is anyone else there?"

"Gawd yes," Marilyn complained. "We're never alone."

"Sit tight then and I'll call you right back." Carolyn started to hang up, then changed her mind. "One more thing, Marilyn."

"Yes?"

"Is it raining in Kansas City?"

Carolyn leaned back on the couch. What was she waiting to be asked to? Nothing. It was her turn to do the asking. He couldn't refuse. Of course the Derby was tomorrow, but he could see his way around that. Especially if she asked.

"Shit!" she said out loud. Thinking about him, she realized that today was Alton's birthday. Carolyn had meant to have him over for a special dinner, even though all he ever talked about was horses. And she'd meant to do something about the gray showing up in her dark hair like spiderwebbing.

ONE

Stupidly, I thought it might be Avery. I'd been sleeping on my face and I knocked over the phone trying to answer it. The couch was supposed to fold out into a bed large enough for two adults. Dream on. In my case, it was too short for one. Reaching from under the covers, blankets stolen from hotel rooms, I located and pulled on the phone cord until I had the receiver in my hand. Someone was already talking.

"What?"

"So, how old are you anyway?" she asked in a rush of false cheerfulness.

Carolyn Sakwoski was the only person in the world I'd let get away with this without cussing. Avery, I foggedly remembered, was the reason I was on the couch in the first place.

"You aren't going to sing, are you?" I mumbled, eyes closed.

"Thirty-five?"

"Hmmm."

"Thirty-six?"

"Four," I said to end the guessing. "Thirty-four."

"Well, you outlived Christ," Carolyn improvised. "Congratulations. Care to start a new religion?"

"Yeah, it's the one where sleep is sacred." I tried to clear my mouth by swallowing every drop of moisture in it.

Carolyn laughed. Then stopped.

"Alton, this is important. Are you awake?"

"No."

"Are you alone?"

"I'm on the couch."

On the couch meant I wasn't alone, but Carolyn misunderstood.

"I have a favor to ask." Her tone held no hint of apology. She sounded as if her favor might involve my doing a little something to save all civilization from imminent ruin rather than to request I feed her dog for a couple days while she was out of town. I'd rather feed the dog.

"Give me a second," I said, turning over on my back to pull myself upright against the scratchy upholstery. I caught my bare shoulder on a button.

"I'm coming over, okay?" she said quickly.

Struggling to concentrate, I waited to hear more. There was no more. She'd already disconnected.

I pictured a man with a long, glistening knife chasing Carolyn around the house. A bloody tear in the bodice of a satin nightgown exposed her heaving breast. I saw myself throwing a lawn chair through the picture window. I couldn't stop picturing her breast. Two a.m. is like that. Before I could kill the guy and make passionate love with my grateful damsel on the kitchen floor, I thought to put the coffee on and unlock the door.

It wasn't long before I was almost standing. Sitting on the edge of the sofa bed, my head between my hands, I stared down at my underwear, startled. They didn't belong to me. Then I recalled they were one of three ridiculous pairs of boxer shorts Avery had given me for my birthday.

"I read in 'Dear Abby' that boxer shorts keep men virile," Avery had said. How the hell did she know what virile meant?

This pair was printed with a pattern of three riderless horses standing behind a railing. Momma Horse, Daddy Horse and Liddle-biddy Baby Horse. It was a perfect world out there on the American horse farm, the family unit serenely intact. I wished I could say the same for my life. Any part of it at any time.

I had every right to be exhausted. I'd shown up at Churchill Downs two hours early to beat the crowd that never materialized, thanks to the rain. I hung around with the diehards and nailed the Kentucky Oaks, my favorite race of the year. Only an idiot bet real money on three-year-old fillies in the slop, but my two picks, a Lukas-trained entry, had stormed in to win and place.

Betting the horses is what I do for a living and what I do to feel alive. Never a dull moment when the rent's out there running in the dirt with a number on his back. I'm almost as good at handicapping as I'd been at stealing cars. The nice part is when you lose at the racetrack, they don't send you to jail. At least, not right away.

Still, sometimes you lose. I lost my wife to further my education. Pregnant with Avery, she filed for divorce while I was earning my laundry-handler's certificate in the McAlester State Pen in Oklahoma. It took me more than ten years to track her down. My daughter, that is. I must have been putting it off, though I didn't realize it at the time.

I am the author of certain crimes. Guess I wanted to be clean of that before I introduced myself to her.

By taking an apartment in Louisville, I devoted the spring of each year to learning to be a father. Of course, I'm also here to go to the track. Spring happens to be the horse-racing season in this part of the country. If my ex-wife had moved to southern California or New York, I could stay in town virtually year-round. Maybe she had thought of that.

I should spend more time with Avery. At thirteen, she has some problems. For one thing, she thinks she's an adult. For another, I'm not certain she likes me, though she's avidly curious about every aspect of my life. Having spent most of her life hating me, she needs some time I suppose to get over that. But most days, she doesn't seem to be trying.

Anyway, the real question was whether Easy Goer could run in the rain. Maybe I'd have to bet the three-year-old colt to show. A good bet for sure, but a lousy way to play the Derby. Rain, though, isn't good for any sport. Unless your game is picking up worms from the sidewalk.

Carolyn came into the apartment without knocking.

"I'm here," she announced, stamping her wet feet on the cruddy orange carpet manufactured exclusively for furnished apartments.

I rose from the couch and watched her shed a plastic raincoat. No torn silk nightgown underneath. No bloodstains. So much for getting what you want on your birth-day.

Carolyn's straight dark hair, cut at the shoulders, was wet. As was much of the rest of her. You have to love Carolyn. She's my best friend. Sometimes when I'm on the road, it seems she is my only friend. The only person I long to talk to.

I save my best stories for her. Stories about horses, trainers, betting coups and jockeys' girlfriends. She never tires of them. In fact, Carolyn says she's going to collect my stories into a book one day, jazz them up a bit and call it *The Inside Track*. The inside track, I figure, is the one around your heart.

I think of Carolyn as widowed, but that's not quite accurate. She and Paul were never married. They lived together, however, for years. Paul Valley was killed in a hunting accident. The hoods who were hunting me murdered him. This was four years ago in Kansas City and I still blame myself for Paul's death. No one has shown up lately to talk me out of it.

Wearing a light-blue sweater and khaki slacks, Carolyn peeled off her soaked jogging shoes. Hers was a long, lean body with square shoulders and ample breasts. Carolyn Sakwoski was the kind of person who, when you gave her a hug, hugged you back. But, generally, she was shy about physical contact.

She pushed both hands through her wet hair, tilting back her head, then reached for the mug of coffee I held out to her.

"This is cold. You have any fresh?"

She was smiling. I hadn't expected that. She looked downright happy, exhilarated.

"And put a shirt on, will you. You know I don't like looking at your tattoo. It's such a stupid thing to have done."

It was nearly 3 a.m. She was lucky that I managed to pull on a pair of jeans and have the bed folded back into a couch.

"Sorry," I said. "But there weren't a large number of entertainment options in prison." I took the mug from her.

"But a rooster? I've never understood that, Alton. Why anyone would have a farm animal tattooed on his body is—"

"It's not a farm animal, Carolyn." I padded barefoot into the kitchenette off the diningette, which was the nearer half of the living-roomette.

"I know, I know. It's a cock," she called after me. "You may as well have had *Let's Fuck* tattooed on your forehead."

"They fight to the death," I explained, returning. "That meant something in prison."

"Oh, come off it. You act like you graduated from Harvard, that having been in prison makes you one of the elite."

"More like MIT," I teased, handing over fresh coffee.

"Well, put a shirt on." She sat on the sofa, sipped her coffee. Carolyn's ears stuck out comically from between plastered locks of wet hair.

"Can't. Avery's in the bedroom."

Carolyn was surprised by the news.

"For the weekend?" she fished.

"Five days. Her mom's in the Bahamas. Be back on Wednesday."

I sat in the chair facing Carolyn and watched her expression change to one of concern. "But you can go ahead and talk," I said. "Avery's a log once she goes to sleep."

"She's thirteen now?"

I nodded. A light came on behind Carolyn's blue eyes. They were looking at me. Eyes take on a different color when they see you.

"You know Avery and I have always got along? She comes in the bookstore when you're out of town."

"I'm glad to hear she gets along with somebody."

"I left some things in the hall," Carolyn said, her eyes flashing off. Setting aside her mug, she stood from the couch and walked in her socks to the door. She slipped into the hall and slipped back in holding a frame, the back of which was splotched with rain.

"Voilà!" she sang, holding it out to me in both hands. "Happy birthday."

It was a Jenness Cortez color etching of last season's Horse of the Year, Alysheba. I'd backed the critter to some advantage in November's Breeders Cup.

"Didn't I see this hanging in the bookstore?" She'd said *some things.* This was one thing. What else was out in the hall?

"I wanted to see if you liked it," Carolyn lied. "I was saving it for your birthday." She propped the framed etching face-first against the wall by the door. "If you didn't, you know, respond to it in a positive way, I wasn't going to give it to you. Give me some credit for planning something in advance, will you?"

I gave Carolyn plenty of credit for planning something in advance. I just wished I knew what it was.

She retrieved her coffee, yet remained standing at the corner of the couch, staring at me with a quizzical intensity.

"I'm tickled to death, Carolyn. It's something I would have chosen for myself." Easily converted to cash, should the need arise, at an art gallery in Lexington I knew of. Cortez's original works had the fine habit of appreciating in value year to year.

"I know that. But what in heaven's name is sticking out of your pants?"

I glanced quickly down and to my own relief found simply that my birthday shorts hit my waist a good two inches above my jeans. You could see the horses peeking out.

"Boxer shorts," I said. "Avery gave them to me. She said I'm supposed to wear them outside my jeans when I'm hanging out at the mall. It would be what she refers to as *rad*."

"It would be radical, all right." Carolyn fiddled with her hair. I waited for her to get around to the real reason for her visit. "It's going to dry like this," she grumbled.

I said nothing.

She looked at me again. "What's on them, lizards?" She leaned forward for a closer look.

"Horses."

"Cute," Carolyn said, then abruptly turned away from me. "Well, birthday or no birthday, that's about all the ass-kissing I have in me. Are you going to help me out or what?"

You had to grin. "You need a place to stay?" I asked, guessing her overnight case might be sitting outside the door.

Carolyn started to talk, then turned on me. "Why would you say *that?*"

"Wishful thinking."

Carolyn made a face. "Don't flirt with me, Alton. We know each other too well for that crap." She was right, but I had the idea she liked it. A little.

If I couldn't say anything nice, I wasn't going to say anything. My mother told me that. Of course, she had more than a few mean things to say in her day herself.

"You remember my sister, Marilyn?"

"She's married to the minor-league pitcher, right?"

"Not anymore."

"Sorry to hear it," I said. "Baseball's tough on marriages."

Was she going to fix me up with Marilyn? Was Marilyn out there in the hall, waiting to be formally introduced to the one man on the planet who could make her new life worthwhile? No one had ever given me a sister for a birthday present.

"Not that, Alton. They're still married. He was called up last year, then came on in spring training and made the Show. That's what Marilyn calls it, the Show."

"The majors," I said.

Carolyn plopped down on the couch. Leaning her back against the arm, she stretched her legs across the cushions. Her slacks were spotted from the knees down with rain.

"The Royals," she said. "He's been through Memphis and Omaha. Had an ERA under 2 in Florida this spring and they signed him on in the bull pen. He's a closer, throws hard stuff."

19

I ran the roster. Tom Gordon. Kevin Appier. Jeff Montgomery. "Not Rowdy Monroe, the blind guy?"

"That's right. Remember, I told you once I was related to Marilyn Monroe and you didn't believe me?"

"You're not going to believe this," I said. "I saw him pitch. Last season, late in the year they called him up when somebody went on the DL. All he had then was a fastball and this incredible bluff."

Carolyn combed both hands through her hair, then shook her head violently from side to side. She grimaced with the result.

"You know," I continued, "once you have the skill, major league pitching is about ninety-percent deception. You can't throw it by them every pitch."

"You can't fool all the batters all the time?"

"Exactly."

"Well, his name's Randall and he's not blind," Carolyn said. She swung her feet from the couch and planted them on the orange expanse of nubby carpet between herself and my chair. Here it comes, I thought.

"Everything went to shit tonight, his whole career. I've been on the phone with Marilyn for hours. They've made two payments on a huge house in the suburbs and it looks like he's going to be sent down. Three earned runs. Then he walked a guy. He got out of the inning when they jerked him for Montgomery. They have a swimming pool and everything. He didn't get a single out, Alton. And I really shouldn't be worrying how my hair looks at a time like this." Carolyn gave her head a final shake.

"He had seven saves in April, Carolyn. According to *USA Today*, the Royals are moving him to middle relief.

He's being groomed for the starting rotation. One bad outing . . ."

"I take that back," she said. "Macfarlane threw out a runner trying to steal second while Randall was on the mound. Randall's contribution to that play was he ducked. See, Alton, all this was based on the money he was going to earn next year—their whole life."

"I know the feeling. Still, they don't send you down for one bad outing."

"You don't understand. He can't pitch anymore! Someone stole his glove earlier today. He can't pitch without it. He has to have it."

"His glove?"

"Actually, they stole his car. But Randall's glove was in the trunk. He can't concentrate without that glove. He's lost his confidence. I know it sounds silly, but it's very real. My poor sister is going to have a nervous breakdown."

Carolyn paused, then pinned me with her crystal-blue eyes. I was already shaking my head no when she said it.

"Alton, we were thinking you might be able to get it back."

"I don't—"

"Marilyn's pregnant."

"I don't see how—"

"Honestly!" Carolyn scowled. "She's married, she's pregnant. Happens all the time."

"I don't see *how* I could help."

"But you can. I know you can."

"I take it the car was stolen in Kansas City?"

"Yes. They're playing a home stand. Otherwise, it

21

would have been in the garage. Oh, Alton, if anybody can help, it's you."

"I could fly to KC, I suppose. But it's already too late. Once a car's gone, well, it's gone." I threw up my hands to make the point.

"That's why we have to hurry," Carolyn urged. "Before they do something with it. Only I thought we could drive. It's ten hours, divided highway all the way. At sixty-five, we could make it in nine, be there by noon," she hurried along. "Even before that. There's the time change. Did I tell you they have a swimming pool? Avery will love it, Alton."

I held up an empty hand to stop her. A conversation traffic cop. With Carolyn, a whistle would have come in handy.

"Obviously, the car was stolen before the game. If it went to a chop shop, it's already in pieces. If it's being sold whole, chances are it's out of town by now. They send them down to Oklahoma to get clean titles."

"What if kids stole it for a joyride and just left the car somewhere with the tags off?"

"It's possible. Where was it stolen from? The ballpark? A restaurant?"

"Their driveway," Carolyn said. "It was taken from the driveway about eight in the morning, maybe eight-thirty. Randall sleeps in. But it was there when Marilyn went out to get the paper, then a little later it was gone. Poof!"

"Poof!" I repeated. I liked that. *Poof!* But cars don't go poof. Dandelion fuzzballs do. Cars get driven, moved indoors, cut into pieces or loaded into trailers and moved

out of the state by the time a stolen-car report can be filed with the police.

Kansas City, being on the state line, is car-thief heaven. With an average of twenty-five cars stolen a day, the Kansas City police are virtually helpless when your car is boosted. They're too busy busting kids who, due to a lack of resources, sell drugs on the street while eighty percent of cocaine transactions take place in executive men's rooms and around desktop computers in air-conditioned offices.

"Nobody steals a car from a driveway in broad daylight, Carolyn, especially when someone's home."

"So it might still be around. You can find it, Alton. Don't you see, you're the only one. The police don't take stolen cars seriously." This was a fact upon which I'd based the success of my earlier career. The cops didn't give a shit, but some judges still took auto theft very seriously. Otherwise, I wouldn't have ended up with this fancy tattoo on my chest.

"And you know the police aren't going to put any effort into finding a baseball glove," Carolyn continued. "And they don't care about Marilyn's marriage, the house payments. Please, Alton. I can help drive. Avery can come with us."

"Hold on." Where did I put that whistle? "It's against the law for me to leave the state with Avery. Judge's orders. They consider it kidnapping, Carolyn. It took me two years to get visitation rights."

"But it's not kidnapping, Alton. She's thirteen. She can make up her own mind."

Avery was born with her mind made up.

"Look, I've got four hundred dollars in emergen

cash at the bookstore. Sarah can see that the money gets put on any horse you want in the Derby. It'll be on TV. You won't miss a thing."

The wind whipped the rain in switches against the window, louder than ever.

"Now, don't you sit there, Alton, and pretend you were going to the track. *Nobody* local goes to the track on Derby day. You can't even get to the windows."

I shook my head glumly. There's no arguing with a woman when her hair is wet.

"Besides, Marilyn can get us really good seats at Royals Stadium. She can get you George Brett's autograph."

"Not Bo Jackson's?" I asked, easing out into the intersection of her conversation. I should have known better.

"Put on a shirt and don't start whining," she snapped. "Technically, your birthday's over."

And so it was.

TWO

My mother once said that truth lives in the last house at the end of the last block in the last town in America. Those were her directions on how not to live your life. "You want the truth, go look for it. You find it, kid, you give me a call."

It was too late to call my mother. Maybe she found something of the truth wherever mothers go when they pass away while you're still in prison. Everyone I loved or cared about disappeared while I was behind bars. That's what jail's for. To keep people from having to say good-bye to you.

I'd dropped off the girls at Carolyn's sister's place without getting out of the van. Had I gone inside and sat down, I'd have been asleep in two minutes. Carolyn looked at me oddly when I told her I wasn't getting out, that I wasn't going to the game. She seemed to have forgotten why we made the trip. Avery, on the other hand, hadn't minded a bit.

Adam White's salvage yard looked a lot like my mother's last house at the end of the last block. But this wasn't quite the last town in America. When I'd last lived in KC, Adam White fenced about half the stolen cars in the area on advance purchase orders from a syndicate of used-car dealers throughout the Midwest. You want to call your used-car dealer a crook, it's okay by me.

"Hey, I know you," Adam White said over the blaring of a portable radio, local coverage of the Saturday afternoon game against Milwaukee. "Buster used to bring you around. You worked Midtown. What's it they call you?"

Even in springtime, these places smell of rancid water and old dogshit. Metal stinks, let me tell you. Even jewelry and especially coins. Autobody parts and twisted grillwork certainly aren't immune. I was known in certain circles by my prison name. But I hadn't come here to refresh an old man's fading memory.

"I'm looking for a car someone stole yesterday. A white convertible Cadillac, maroon top, upholstery and rear-wheel cover. Gold trim. You wouldn't have heard of anybody towing in a car like this one?"

"You sound like a cop, son," White said.

"You know better than that. The owner needs to find the car is all. They asked me to check around."

"Somebody paying to get it back?"

"That's not the deal," I told him. "They don't want the car. There's medicine locked in the trunk. An inhaler, too. A six-year-old boy needs regular medication to be able to breathe."

"So do I," old man White interrupted, starting to laugh. "Only my medicine comes in pints, you know what I mean?"

He meant liters. "Asthma," I went on. "This kid's

26

down with it all the time. And the boy wants his baseball glove. It's special to him."

I didn't care if the old fart believed me. I only wanted to get the message across. Adam White was in his seventies now and mostly retired, according to the fine people I'd spoken with at Bob Eulitt's junkyard just outside the city limits on the other side of town.

"Medicine wouldn't be drugs? You ain't talking about drugs to me, are you?"

"No. I was hoping you'd give a rat's ass about a sick kid. All I really want is the baseball glove. Pete LaCock gave it to the boy a couple years back when the kid was in the hospital. It's a big deal to him, this glove. There'd be no questions asked, no follow-up. I can see to that."

"How much?"

"Two hundred," I said flatly. He'd either care that the youngster got the glove back or not. Price was irrelevant except that there had to be one. Nothing's free in the underground economy. Hell, nothing's free. Period.

White leaned back in his dilapidated chair that the post office must have thrown out in the 1930s. A greasy tool counter passed for the desk in the salvage-yard office. The old man still wore oil in his hair and his face looked like something God had made up while experimenting with sealing caulk. Sooner or later and that shit cracks.

The old man let me wait while he thought it over. The Royals were up two-zip. Saberhagen was on the mound. I hoped Carolyn and Avery were enjoying themselves at the ballpark while missing out on all this smelly fun.

"I don't do business with a person don't tell me his name," White finally said.

"Rooster," I informed the gent.

27

"Rooster, yeah. That was it. Let's see, you got a tattoo or something the other, don't you? A real big pretty one?"

I undid the top four buttons of my plaid shirt and showed the old man my chest. He barely glanced at it, then reached over to turn the radio down. I heard shuffling in the back room. An outside door opened and closed. I hoped they weren't leaving on my account.

"Heard you left town *for a reason,*" White said.

"Guess I've got one for coming back. The baseball glove belongs to a friend of a friend, you see what I'm saying?"

"All my friends are dead, mister. I don't owe nobody no favors. You got a tag number?"

"How many maroon-over-white Cadillac convertibles get towed in during the week? This one was taken yesterday."

"It was towed, was it?" As many cars are stolen in Kansas City by tow trucks as are hot-wired and driven off from unattended all-day parking lots.

"It wasn't a key man," I said to make my point. A key man is a thief who specializes in stealing the keys to a car, either from a dealership or an open purse in a crowded bar, before driving it to the marketplace.

"I know this is foreign to your ears, son. But sometimes a person steals a car to get somewhere in it. They drive it there and they leave it there."

"Nobody steals a new Cadillac from a driveway to visit their mother in Maggody, Arkansas. It got left somewhere, it was probably here in town," I said. "Some kid abandoned it and maybe it was picked up on a tow." I couldn't accuse White of having stolen the car and expect his help.

"Maybe," he said. "That happens sometimes. You got the license-plate number?"

"I thought perhaps you'd notice a car like this one." I was losing my patience.

"I got a clipboard full of numbers is what I got, Rooster. I got two more yards where cars are sittin'. A paved lot on Troost. What's the plate?"

"Missouri," I capitulated. "Personalized tag. ASA-BAT. Ay-Ess-Ay-Bee-Ay-Tee."

"Say again? What's that mean?"

"As a bat. Guy wears glasses, he's nearly blind."

"I don't get it."

I couldn't explain it to him. It was a good one, though, for a major league fastballer. Besides his reputation as a blind-boy pitcher, the tag worked another way. A bat that couldn't find the ball didn't get a hit, no matter whose beefy shoulder it rested on.

Adam White cocked his large head sideways. "Got a car in the other day with the damnedest plate. R-U-1-2. Took us a hell of a long time to figure it. R-U-1-2. You know, Are You One Too? The guy was Italian, it turned out."

I thought there might be more to it than being Italian.

"Asabat," White continued. "A Caddy. I got nothin' like that. You try Cory's place?"

"He's next on my list," I lied.

"Tell Cory hello for me, huh, Rooster? You understand what I'm saying? Tell him I said hello and maybe he can help."

"Yeah, right."

"And welcome back, son. You get something you want to sell, bring it by. You hear me?" Adam White attempted a wide smile. It looked like the old fence was trying to spit his teeth across the room.

Mom was right. There wasn't much truth around this place. You couldn't trust Adam White's radio to give the correct score of the ball game. Stepping out of the oily office onto the gravel lot with its unhealthy mix of rusty pieces of wire, nuts and bolts, I realized I was getting the answers I'd anticipated. Had Rowdy Monroe's car been parked at Adam White's house, the old man would be mouthing the same saw.

For Carolyn's sake, I'd go through the motions, taking blind swings at imaginary curves without a bat in my hands. I sucked in the sunshine, of which there was plenty in Kansas City, and looked around. One year's vintage junk was as bad as another's. Salvage yards always look like dead rodeos to me.

You had to watch where you were walking or the stink would trip you up. Shuffling the gravel under my shoes awoke the old aroma. Everything smelled worse since I quit smoking. Kansas City just happened to be today's olfactory offense. I opened the door of my van to a huddled surprise.

A small man crouched down in front of the passenger's seat, hiding. I climbed into my seat, staring at the stowaway as you would stare at your feet in the middle of the day when you notice your socks don't match.

"Don't let 'em see me," the fellow hissed in a forced whisper. I was unthreatened by the man's presence because it wasn't a man at all. It was a kid.

I closed my door to keep from picking up more flies. Why would they want to leave a place like this?

"Running away from home?" I asked, starting the van.

"Suck the steam off my shorts," the kid said. "I know who you are and I got what you want."

THREE

After checking the rear of the van for accomplices, I eased it across the ruts. Once we were on the highway, I turned off the radio. The youthful intruder pulled himself into the passenger's seat and peered nervously into the side-mounted mirror.

The boy had black hair cropped exceedingly short. The back of the burr cut was shaved into an oval that looked like a loose-toothed jack-o'-lantern. He wore a red leather jacket over a black T-shirt tucked into the usual pair of jeans with horizontal gashes at the knees. Only this kid's were cuffed. He was about the size of any of my favorite jockeys.

"A smart mouth is a bad habit," I said.

"Bad habits is my middle name. You want the baseball mitt or not?"

"Speaking of names, I don't believe we've been introduced."

"You want the mitt, get on Twenty-third Street and keep going west."

The kid wouldn't look at me, but kept a careful eye out the side window.

"I have a bad habit myself," I said. "I don't drive places just because people tell me to." Carolyn had, after all, said please. I pushed the console button that locked the doors.

"So let me out and I'll walk."

"That's precisely what I had in mind." I slid the van into the exit lane and rolled off the ramp and onto I-435 north. "I was thinking maybe the Iowa state line. You ever been to Iowa in the spring?"

I turned the radio back on, listening for the score at Royals Stadium.

"I take it you don't want the glove," my passenger said over the called third strike on Danny Tartabull.

"Guess not."

The inning was over and we were leaving town, me and my boy companion.

"You serious?"

"I don't care about the glove. All I cared about was looking for the glove. I was doing someone a favor. Said I'd ask around. I never even met the guy who lost it. See, a close friend of mine had the rainy-day blues. She needed a small vacation so, well, I drove her here."

I clicked off the radio. "You may as well tell me your name."

"You're bluffing."

"I seriously doubt it."

"I ain't walking from no Iowa!"

I think that's on their state seal. "Who told you life was easy?" I asked. "Your name, please."

"Robin Bunter. They call me Bird. Like a rooster's a bird, you know."

"Don't get smart," I warned him. I don't like being called Rooster so virulently that I'd been considering having a sailor suit tattooed over the multicolored feathers of the fighting cock on my chest and calling myself Donald Duck.

"Look," the kid said, "I know who you are. You got a reputation here. Old man White used to talk about you. Said you was the only boost he knew that never got caught. Said other stuff too."

"I don't boost anymore, junior. It's a dead end." I changed lanes. "So, Robin Bird Bunter, do you have a driver's license or something you can show me?"

"I got three," he said, eager to duel.

"None of them yours. I know. I know what else you have. A juvenile arrest record, no doubt. Both states?"

"I'm better than that now," Bird insisted. "I have certain talents. Besides, I don't do diddly on the Kansas side. Hey, why don't you turn this thing around?"

"How old are you?"

"Old enough to drive. You getting tired?"

I looked at Bird more closely. The kid wasn't shaving yet. "You aren't old enough to drive."

"Up yours!"

"Fifteen?"

Bird shook his head, refusing to reply. His mute response was as good as an answer.

"You're not even fifteen yet?"

"Next month, all right!" Then he tried to defend himself. "I did forty-three cars so far this year alone. I did one today, that's why I needed a ride. The old fart told me to wait till they had a tow call. I hate those damn trucks, they ruin your clothes just looking at them. Come on now, turn this thing around!"

"Okay. Let's get that baseball glove and then maybe I'll buy you an ice cream cone."

"I should have known you'd be a total asshole."

Beats the hell out of being a total idiot. "Now, now," I said paternally. "Be nice and I won't ask you what that is cut into the back of your head. And, if you're real polite, maybe I'll introduce you to my daughter."

It was meant as a joke. But as I said it I was stung by the idea that Avery was old enough to consort with professional criminals. Not a happy notion. Must have been the same notion that Avery's mother got into her head when she decided to divorce me and head for the hills while I was completing my vocational training at McAlester.

"Sure thing," Bird said, fighting back. "She got big hooters, or what?"

I slammed on the brakes, pitching the kid from the seat. A cloud of dust rose from the van as it careened to a dead stop on the crushed-rock shoulder of the four-lane. Bird cursed as he straightened himself in his seat. I stared at the punk with heated intensity until, finally, he looked back at his gone-berserk driver.

"That's one mistake," I informed him solemnly. And, without a break in tone or the slightest falter to my unblinking stare, I added, "Let's not make another one."

"Hey, man, don't rupture something," Bird said, his voice quaking.

Avery was my soft spot. We didn't meet until she was nearly twelve. Now, two years later, I tried very hard not to love her too much. For her part, Avery did everything in her power to keep that from happening. Yet, as far as I was concerned, the real world, the harsh one, was strictly off-limits for my daughter. She had to know it was there, sure; but I wasn't about to let it touch her, not ever.

There were no heavy-metal rock posters, no magazine photos of hot rods, no *Playboy* centerfolds tacked up on the walls of Bird's apartment. No model airplanes, ships or cars, and no sports paraphernalia anywhere. You couldn't smell a hamster. His walk-up on Linwood Boulevard didn't look like a place where a kid lived, except that it was furnished in such bad taste.

Bird was an awkward host. We stood inside the door as if tied on strings, waiting for the other to move or say something. I spied an uncomfortable-looking red plastic couch from a safe distance and decided to remain standing. The chair across from it was cheap Mediterranean with shiny black cushions that looked wet.

What Bird lacked in taste he made up for with expensive electronic gear, including a forty-eight-inch rear-projection television screen and console. Plastic shelves along the other wall held a glistening array of components, in the middle of which sat a very expensive CD player. The shelves were guarded at either end by a cabinet speaker larger than Reverend Jim Bakker's air-conditioned doghouse.

Once he was through watching me watch the room, I followed Bird around a glass-and-chrome dining table and into the apartment's one bedroom. Bird walked past the bed and into the bathroom. I heard the door lock.

I picked up the Radio Shack telephone next to the king-size waterbed with a black crushed-velvet cover and pushed the asterisk for the hell of it. Using other people's automatic re-dial button had become an errant hobby of mine. It rang four times and then someone answered the phone.

"Jim" was all he said. There was a noise in the background like someone dropping a truck off a three-story building.

The huge waterbed challenged three walls against the placement of additional furniture in the room. Bird, though, had managed to line up four three-drawer dressers along the wall with the apartment's only window. The dressers were painted bright red. An upright Hoover occupied the corner where another kid might pile his shoes and dirty clothes.

"Don't tell me," I said when Bird came back. "Shirts." I pointed. "Sweaters?" I pointed at the next dresser. "Socks and underwear . . . and jeans?"

"T-shirts," Bird said. "I like them folded." He tossed his head toward the white accordion doors of the bedroom closet. "Jeans are in there. I like them on hangers."

This was one strange kid.

"Where's the ironing board?" Actually, I was wondering where were the stamp collection, the baseball cards, the Nintendo games and the fishbowl with a turtle in it.

"No way," Bird said. "I send my stuff out. How much for the mitt?"

I scratched my chin.

"How much for the mitt?" he repeated.

"I was thinking you give it to me for the ride over."

"You're kidding, right? You don't drive all over town

asking about a stolen Caddy if you aren't going to pay for the mitt."

"Fifty bucks," I offered.

"That's the same as free," he protested.

"No it's not. Fifty bucks is fifty bucks. Free is when I slap you in the mouth and take the glove with me."

"I got a gun. You should know that."

"Look, kid, why'd you bring me up here? You could have run up and brought it down. I'd pay you your fifty up front."

Bird shook his head. "Five hundred."

"You hurting for company, Bird? Is that it?"

Bird jerked away from the conversation and pulled open the closet door. He retrieved the baseball glove and threw it at me from inside the closet. It weighed more than I'd expected. And instead of being tan-colored it was black. The glove smelled of oil and sweat.

"You can have the fucking thing," Bird said, rummaging through the closet.

"You brought me up here to approve of all this," I said, feeling like a father. "To show someone how all grown-up you are. That you're a big-time professional crook. Well, I sure as hell ain't no role model, Bird. I don't think you should spend your life stealing cars. Hear me? I think you should be in school."

"Who said you were a hero?" Bird emerged from the closet, holding something. He grinned. "I got some other business here I wanted to see about."

He held up a videocassette for my brief inspection. It had a yellow label with a red circle. I trailed him back into the front room, massaging Rowdy Monroe's baseball glove in both hands. Miracle accomplished, thank you.

I'd have to have new business cards printed. Maybe I could heal the sick. You never know.

Bird plugged the tape into the player but didn't turn it on. Instead, he strode into the kitchenette, a businessman's stern expression on his face. Playing adult was the only way this juvenile delinquent seemed to have any fun.

"You want a beer?" he called from the fridge. "Or a glass of wine? I got white."

"Beer's fine. You buy that stuff yourself?"

"Were you born a dweeb or what?" Dweeb was one of Avery's words.

A kid who has three driver's licenses can have any date of birth he wants, I figured. He handed me a cold bottle of beer on his way to the plastic shelves, where he picked up the remote and pointed it. The television came loudly to life.

It was a homemade video shot in a hotel room. A woman was naked on a bed. She clutched the bare buttocks of a man standing at the bed's edge. Her head bobbed in front of the man's crotch. Red fingernails appeared to press deep holes into the man's baby-white and muscled ass. Only the edges of her dark hair came into view on the upstrokes.

The camera was stationary without a change in focus. Probably on a tripod. Or a small videocam hidden in a shoebox on the shelf of the closet with the door left open.

The fourteen-year-old hit fast-forward, drinking his beer with one eye closed as if to take steady aim with the remote control. He punched pause as the woman lay on the bed, the man caught in mid-crawl between her spread legs lifted slightly at the knees.

"Know who that is?" Bird asked.

Her face was in full view. She looked to be in her early thirties, pretty enough, even held in mid-flicker.

"Well?" my host urged. "Look close."

"Nobody I'd care to meet," I finally said, wondering if I were lying.

"Dorothy Fleming," the kid car-thief said with a touch of reverence in his voice.

The name wasn't totally unfamiliar. "The ice skater?"

"Naw man," Bird said, wishing I could have recognized her so I might share in his awe. "Dorothy Fleming. She had that affair with the Toronto baseball guy, Ray Twiggs."

"Right." Now it came to me. She'd carried on with quite a few major leaguers. Fleming had asked Twiggs for a large sum of money when he tried to break it off. Instead of paying, he'd gone to the Mounties screaming blackmail. For a while, Fleming had been in all the magazines, including a nude layout in one of the male-marketed periodicals, and on all the talk shows, cashing in on her fifteen minutes of fame Andy Warhol promised us all.

I stared at the tall man on the screen for a moment more. It wasn't Twiggs. For one thing, this guy wore glasses.

"Turn it off," I said. I finished my beer and sat it on Bird's plastic table, taking Rowdy's glove in both hands again.

"Where'd you get it?" I asked, but I already had an idea.

"Same place I got that mitt you're wearing. In the trunk of the Caddy. I always run the trunks and glove boxes before I drive 'em in."

Bird hit rewind. "She's at the Regal Inn across from the ballpark," he added.

"How do you know?"

"I'm not stupid. I called there and asked for her. It's where the ballplayers hang out. It was a longshot, but I struck pay dirt. Six thousand dollars' worth. Not bad, huh?"

"You're selling it back to her?"

"Sure. I bring it to her room—let's see, it's 931—during today's game, and she pays me six grand."

"You talked to her then?"

"Right."

"So what's the catch, kid? Why bring me in? You want to brag, is that it?"

Of course he wanted to brag. It was a hell of a bonus, six grand. Bird was shaking his head sadly, as if I couldn't be counted on to understand anything.

"You think I'm going to buy it?" I finally asked.

"No."

"Why not, Bird? I wanted the glove. I know whose car it is. I might want the tape. Maybe you can get another five hundred off me."

"It's a done deal." Bird was agitated. "I thought you might, well, sort of back me up, you know? Maybe she's setting me up. Maybe that guy on the tape is going to be there waiting . . ."

"Now you're thinking, kid. Did you look at all of it?"

Bird nodded.

"Nobody but those two on the tape?"

"She does a solo act. Other than that, it's just Romeo and Juliet. I had to act fast, you know, to get the money. I didn't get that much for the car. So, it's not perfect or anything, the exchange. I thought if I gave you the glove for nothing you could come along with the tape. I'd go up and get the money. That way they can't do anything funny."

I didn't want to know the tape existed. You stand there long enough and people will tell and show you things you never wanted to hear or see. People's private lives should be kept private.

"You know who Rowdy Monroe is, don't you?" I asked.

"Yeah, sure."

"Why didn't you sell it to him? It's his bare butt all over the video."

"You can't get those guys on the phone. Besides, I didn't want to blackmail nobody. I'm just selling it back to her."

"Well, she *might* pay you, Bird."

"What you mean?"

"For all she knows, you made a copy. She's not going to fork over six grand. That's to get you up there with the tape in your sweaty little hands. She'll have somebody with her, you can count on it. And they're going to try to scare the shit out of you. Maybe start breaking your fingers with a pair of pliers, something like that. To, you know, get your cooperation. Maybe you can convince them you didn't make a copy before they start on your other hand."

"Back me up then!"

I shook my head.

"You want half? Is that it?"

"I don't want a damn thing to do with it, kid. That's the truth. What I think you should do is let me drive you out there and you leave the tape at the desk for Miss Fleming and be done with it. You didn't tell her your name or anything stupid, did you?"

"And walk away empty-handed? No thanks, Rooster. I'll call a cab."

FOUR

Bird and I kept talking. I wanted the tape returned to Dorothy Fleming. It was my way out of this little mess. If I kept the tape, even buying it from young Robin Hood, I'd have to give it back to Rowdy. It would require a confrontation with Carolyn's family. I had enough confrontation in my own family. In Avery's mind, the only difference between a thirteen-year-old schoolgirl and a twenty-three-year-old college woman is her father. And she never lets me forget it.

A person pays for his mistakes. It's the way we learn. If Fleming were holding the tape over Rowdy's head, who was I to intercede in his education? Perhaps Rowdy was going to learn this lesson twice because of me. Perhaps he'd already paid for the tape. But it was pretty much the way things were going to be, whether or not I had driven to Kansas City.

I sat in the van in the parking lot and fidgeted. I had about an hour before the horses left the gates at Churchill. I'd watch it on the small television in the van if need be. I'd boxed Carolyn's four hundred dollars on an exacta of Sunday Silence and Easy Goer. They were the only two horses in the race.

Time moved at a crawl. In the bottom of the seventh, the Royals were onto a three-run lead and it looked as if Saberhagen would complete the game.

There's a button in the human mind that presses itself when enough time has finally lapsed that you're certain what you're waiting for isn't coming. My button always rings a bell. You learn to listen for it. The first time a woman is stood up on a date, she might not hear it ringing for an hour and a half, two hours, three. A couple more times, and she hears it ringing its ass off in fifteen minutes. In my case, it sounds like an alarm clock going off inside an aluminum pan some fool placed on my pillow while I was sleeping.

The kid had ditched me. It was hard to miss.

I jumped out of the van, slammed the door, and made my way inside the Regal Inn.

"Room 931," I told one of the uniformed desk clerks. "Someone was supposed to leave a package for me. I'm Fleming."

The clerk left and returned. He was sorry. There were no messages for Room 931.

I rode the empty, nearly silent elevator to the ninth floor of the hotel across from the Truman Sports Complex. You could see into Royals Stadium from the upper suites that had windows facing southwest. The hotel had been built with that in mind, and guests paid a fancy premium for rooms facing the ballpark on game days. The Regal Inn was also the hotel where most of the visiting teams stayed. I wouldn't be surprised if a secret tunnel led under the highway from the hotel to the stadium.

The maid's cart was at the end of the hall. I pocketed a handful of complimentary chocolates out of habit and tapped on the open door of the room she was cleaning. I walked in. I walked out seconds later behind the purposeful march of the matronly woman in a starched uniform.

No one answered her knock at Room 931. I hadn't had time to dicker and had dropped a C-note to make certain the maid had ample reason not to remember me if she were later asked. She opened 931 with her passkey and pivoted away from the door without a glance in my direction.

Perhaps Dorothy Fleming had gone to the game.

My hand on the knob, I held the door ajar until the maid had trekked by several rooms between 931 and her cart at the end of the hall. Then I pushed it open and called out, "Hello? Anybody home?"

I thought I heard something move inside the room, but I must have been mistaken. The only one in Room 931 was Dorothy Fleming. And she was dead.

Anything but lovely in bed, the woman's eyes bulged in a questioning, unfocused stare. Her expression seemed to be asking me what the hell I was doing there. Good question.

Dorothy Fleming's mouth was open far too widely. She looked to be choking on something. Death *is* hard to swallow. Mostly, though, she looked surprised. The bullet hole was in her forehead, placed neatly above one eye.

There was less blood than you might expect. She'd died quickly. This Dorothy certainly wasn't in Kansas anymore. Or any other state in our glorious union you could name.

I stood in the middle of the room, massaging my fore-head with two fingers. Dorothy was dressed in some-thing unattractive that older women wear to dinner when there is no one to impress. Somewhere over the rainbow, I thought, rubbing harder, was a pot of golden piss and I'd stepped right into the stinking middle of it.

My brain screamed at me to shake a leg. Bird had said he had a gun was my other thought.

Of course, this was all Carolyn's fault. I should have been in Louisville, watching my bet run a muddy circle around the track. Instead, I turned slowly in place at the foot of Dorothy's bed and surveyed the room. Oh, the doo-dah day.

Clothes were draped over one of the two chairs. Half-finished drinks and the ice bucket were on the table. A Kansas City *Star* lay in sections across the floor. There was a clutter of toiletries on the low dresser, a small scat-tering of jewelry, an unopened box of tampons. And her purse, rigid with the little secrets all purses contain, sat next to a wadded, damp towel.

There were two television sets, one where it should be. The other occupied a four-legged cart, on a shelf above a videocassette player. It had been unplugged from the wall and flashed *12:00, 12:00, 12:00* like a traffic light gone bananas. Blood-red bananas. The tape had been ejected but was still in place. It should be dusted for fingerprints, no doubt.

The maid would remember me. A hundred bucks was no longer enough for her to keep her mouth shut. But there was a chance her own fear of repercussions for hav-ing broken the rules to let someone into an occupied room where a guest was murdered would keep her from talking. On my way out, I snatched up the hotel towel and wiped the doorknob. Down the hallway, I let the towel fall to the carpet, the videocassette of Dorothy Fleming's sexual tricks tucked neatly in my armpit.

The spot on my forehead throbbed. The elevator doors opened before I got there. A small, neatly dressed man rushed out. A plaid wool sweater under a beige blazer. His face was red with exertion or worry. I couldn't tell which. I slipped into the vacant elevator before the fellow could turn around to look at me.

Bird had just made my all-time A-one official shitlist. Until I'd met Avery not so long ago, I believed a mere youngster was entirely incapable of accomplishing such an extraordinary distinction. Now I was beginning to understand that the youth of America was capable of all manner of personal achievement.

But was Bird capable of murder? The type of murder where you place a small-caliber handgun to someone's head and fire a single shot? Wouldn't Dorothy have simply slapped the gun out of his hand and told him to behave?

Descending in the elevator did nothing to loosen the tangle of knots in my stomach. A wise man at this point would put his van on I-70 and keep it there until he grew lost in the hundreds of miles of dark prairie west of town. Kansas City is an easy place to escape from if you don't mind ending up nowhere in particular.

I, however, had obligations to keep. Having a daughter does things to a man that make him have to stick around.

FIVE

The ball game was over and I was exhausted. The Kentucky Derby had come and gone. Wathan didn't use the bull pen. Bo Jackson hit a solo home run in the bottom of the eighth. Easy Goer screwed up early in the slop at Churchill Downs, then came on late to be up for place behind Sunday Silence's impressive win. My exacta earned a handsome profit.

I fell asleep on the customized bench-bed in the back of the van, worrying about murder. I didn't like the idea that live people were turned into dead people with their eyes wide open. I didn't like the idea that Dorothy Fleming, though dead, had seen me looking at her tampons.

Those damn tampons had somehow made her murder personal, a private affair I was party to merely because I was dumb enough to be there. Hell, it was like I was married to her. Women ought to keep those things in their purses, or under something in a bathroom drawer. I felt as if I'd been caught doing something horribly wrong, irredeemably wrong. Just by being there. I'd been caught looking and I was beginning to really hate this town.

I woke to Carolyn's banging on the sliding side-door of the van. They were home from the game. She helped me carry the bags into the house, which looked like a small Ramada Inn. It was one of those monster homes realtors call contemporary Tudor executive or contemporary Georgian executive or, hell, just executive.

"Four-plus bedrooms and three and a half baths," Carolyn told me.

It seemed bigger. "What's a plus-bedroom is what I want to know." A half bath is when you forget to wash your feet.

"In this case, it's a sitting area off the master suite. And a fireplace."

"Gee, I thought a plus-bedroom meant you could put a roll-away bed on the back porch if you had to."

Monroe Manor sat on an acre of lawn with three trees somebody must have bussed in to make the sale. Two wide and double-gabled stories, the lower one brick, faced front. The basement opened at yard level in the back of the house to a redwood deck six inches above the dirt. The deck surrounded an in-ground swimming pool and a snazzy little hot tub elevated off to one side.

Carolyn led me on a casual tour and I saw for myself what "plus" means in today's real estate market—that it takes an additional clause to describe each room sufficiently. There wasn't a simple sentence structure in the place.

"You need to bring along a canteen," I said, "to check whether all the windows are locked."

"Here it is. I hope you don't mind," Carolyn said.

She opened the door to an upstairs bedroom that over-looked the front lawn. This one, too, had a fireplace. There were two pine dressers and a matching wardrobe, a walk-in closet and a bathroom, but only one double bed and that was the problem Carolyn hoped I didn't mind.

"There are other people in the house, Alton. Rowdy's brother and three of his friends are here for the weekend. Avery gets the hide-a-bed in the rumpus room on the ground level."

"Just you, me, and the moonlight?" I sat down her suitcase and my duffel bag.

"I figure we can manage it. If you think something clumsy might happen in your sleep, you can always bed down in the back of your van."

"What are friends for?"

"We're both adults, Alton."

"Right you are."

"So tell me, did you find it?"

"I couldn't find the car," I told the truth.

Carolyn attempted a momentary look of concern, yet it was obvious she had little emotion invested in Rowdy Monroe's vehicular loss. I would decide later whether to tell anyone I had the glove. I wanted to talk with Rowdy about that. I was certain I'd mention the video to no one. Both glove and video were stashed in the van.

"I met the strangest kid, Carolyn. A fourteen-year-old car thief. An ace."

"Sounds like someone I know. This way," she guided. "To the ground floor. I hope pizza's okay with you. Marilyn didn't feel like cooking. It took us a while to figure out you were in the van. It should be here any minute."

"He's smarter than I ever was at that age," I continued. "Seems fairly successful. Full-time pro and he doesn't have a driver's license. He's fourteen, Carolyn, and has his own apartment."

"That's sad. I thought it was against the law for minors not to have guardians. Don't they put them on state farms or something? By the way, Avery went with the boys after the game. I hope it's all right with you. She's so excited, Alton, I thought it might be fun."

"Boys?"

"Rowdy and his brother, those guys. Marilyn didn't want to go along. They're going to ride the new roller coaster at Worlds of Fun, the wooden one. Don't you love this house?"

Two rooms opened onto the deck around the swimming pool. The one we hiked through, the rumpus room, was obviously Rowdy's. It was lined with trophy cases, one end centered by an eight-foot slate pool table. There was a couch group in the middle and two weight machines at the other end, in front of the fireplace in the back wall. I wouldn't mind having a percent of the log concession around this place.

Rowdy Monroe's Topps baseball card from last year had been enlarged to poster size, framed and hung above the fireplace mantel. If they had bubblegum cards for thieves, Bird would have earned a Rookie-of-the-Year card.

Two more rooms completed the ground level. One, with its own sliding glass doors to the deck, was outfitted with plants and white wicker chairs. There were thick red towels on a white, wrought-iron stand. I followed Carolyn through this room and into a comfortably large sitting room, complete with bookcases, fireplace, and a beautiful woman sitting on the sofa.

There had to be a washer and dryer somewhere. Doesn't every basement have them? Maybe they dried their clothes on racks in front of the fireplaces after running them through the cycle on the hot tub.

"Oh hi." Marilyn Sakwoski Monroe didn't look pregnant to me.

"This is Alton," Carolyn said.

"Nice to meet you, Alton." Marilyn sat aside a leather-bound notebook she'd been writing in when we'd entered the room. She lay her pen on the coffee table, next to a tumbler of melting ice, an ashtray and a pack of menthol cigarettes.

"I'm sorry," she said, standing in a thick-pile terry cloth bathrobe with pink piping. "Seeing my sister after all this time inspired me."

She held out her hand. I accepted it. I'd seen her before, standing in the front drive when I'd dropped off Carolyn and Avery. And maybe, just maybe, she'd been on the cover of *Sports Illustrated*'s swimsuit issue. Marilyn was younger than Carolyn and blonde, with slightly less of an overbite, which gave her lips a full, kissable look.

Marilyn wore the same blue eyes as her older sister. If she were pregnant, it had to be all of three days, and I certainly wouldn't have minded having a hand in it.

"Marilyn writes poetry," Carolyn said.

"Well, that's . . ." I began and lost my place. "That's, uh, interesting." I tried a sincere expression.

"She's taking classes at the University," Carolyn added. "With, uh . . ."

"Michael Heffernan," Marilyn said brightly. "He's

published three books and has a Ph.D. in American Literature. He thinks I've got what it takes."

No argument there. But as far as I was concerned, all the really good poets worked at Hallmark Cards. *Too bad, Jack, you had to fall. Rest up, get well, have a ball.*

"Marilyn's interested in the human soul," Carolyn said without laughing.

I nodded. Sincerely.

Marilyn smiled to herself.

"But only as it surfaces in certain feelings," she said. "You see, I'm interested in internal damage control and the images that rise as healing entities, after and during inner turmoil and conflict. What I'm after is a pure image of peace and harmonic revelation which can be turned to in times of utter angst. Like, you know, when you're dying. It may take years. Right now I'm tuning the inner ear and working with intuitive leaps."

I nodded my ass off.

"A good deal of life has nothing to do with reality. Outer reality, I mean," Marilyn explained.

"The weather?" I tried.

"Exactly," Marilyn said. "I'm going to take a tub, if you don't mind answering the door when the pizza comes." She picked up her cigarettes and ashtray and waltzed into the wicker room. I heard the glass door slide open and, for the life of me, could only think of a tub of fried chicken.

"Don't say a word," Carolyn warned. "She's very smart."

"A tub?"

"The hot tub, Alton."

"She didn't mention the glove."

"Marilyn wants to talk to you alone." Carolyn rolled her eyes. "She's afraid you might not be entirely honest with her in front of me."

"We're not what you'd call a harmonic entity?"

"Now, Alton."

"Hey, I like poetry." I'd picked up more than a little verse in prison. "I'm interested in the human soul."

"Alton, I'm warning you . . ."

"There once was a miner named Dave," I began, right hand clutching my chest. "Who kept a dead whore in a cave."

"That's enough."

"He was a bit of a twit, you have to admit," I rushed. "But look at the money he saved."

"You think that's funny?"

"After or during periods of utter angst?"

"Shut up," Carolyn begged, laughing. "You can be such a shit!"

"How are you holding up?"

"I'm beat. After the pizza comes I'm going to bed. You might take a piece out to Marilyn. It'll give you a chance to talk." As if on cue, the doorbell rang. I paid for the pizza. Carolyn showed me the kitchen, one floor above the rumpus room. It opened onto a narrow, elevated deck that overlooked the swimming pool.

I found a Boulevard Pale Ale in the refrigerator. Somebody had good taste. Boulevard Pale was one hundred percent malted barley with a heavier body and more flavor than regular American beers. Yet it avoided the thick, slimy feel of commercial imports. The rich, smooth beer was my favorite drink this side of scotch, just one side or the other of being sober.

Marilyn was still in the hot tub by the time I got out there. The hot tub was off to one side, close to the house. I carried one of the boxed pizzas and two beers with me. Marilyn's bathrobe was on the redwood bench that encircled the elevated tub. The water bubbled ferociously and was brightly lighted from the inside. The sky was turning dark.

Her hair was wet and still she was beautiful. She was also naked. I noticed it too late and for the longest time stood over her—caught looking again. Maybe it was only a second or two but it seemed like a long time. She turned a switch and the water smoothed. She smiled up at me.

I sat the pizza on the edge of the tub and held out a beer to her. Then I sat down on the rim of the tub, my back to her.

"I wanted to talk with you alone," she said, climbing out. "I hope you don't mind." I heard her set the bottle on the bench. She wrapped her wet body back into her robe, which soaked up every inch of it.

"I'm a private person." Marilyn sat on the bench, patting the space next to her. "Most poets are."

I hopped off the edge of the tub, removed a slice of cooling pizza and got some into my mouth. Marilyn hadn't belted her robe and most of one white breast was saying hello to me. I'd seen the pose before, but I couldn't nail down the specific dream.

"I didn't find the car," I said, turning away from her.

"Sit down," she suggested. "I want to talk."

I am a born stander. Ask my mother. It made people nervous. It made school difficult. But I enjoy standing, shifting my weight, leaning against things. It's how I relax. I'm never comfortable sitting next to anyone.

"I'm sorry," I said. "It was a longshot. I checked all the places I know to check."

"I didn't really think you would find it," Marilyn said. "Carolyn seemed so, well, avid about it."

"She wanted to see you."

"Do you know how old I am?"

I swallowed the last of my slice, shaking my head.

"Twenty-eight. Do you know how old Carolyn is?"

"More or less," I admitted.

"She's more than a dozen years older than I am. Carolyn's much more than a sister to me. She's someone I've always looked up to. She's very, very smart, you know. Too smart for most men."

What did this have to do with anything?

"She seems, I don't know, so lonely. When she was living with that ex-convict, I tried everything to break it up. It wasn't good for her."

That ex-convict happened to have been my best friend. Marilyn hadn't touched her pizza.

"But when he died, Carolyn changed. She opened her bookstore in Louisville because that's where he was from."

I was nearly through my second slice.

"She went off the deep end. She crossed over the edge, you see. Carolyn doesn't seem to be having any fun in her life. She seems very lonely."

"She does?"

"You know, Carolyn really likes your daughter. I think that's very good for her. But there's something big missing in her life, I'm afraid. She's getting older and she's all alone."

Utter angst, I thought. Marilyn didn't know her big sister very well. But who was I to talk? I was on the road most of the year.

"Sit down, *please*," Marilyn said. "And tell me what your intentions are with my sister. Are you stringing her along?"

The night darkened dramatically. Marilyn Monroe's eyes drilled me with a brilliant flash, like blue lights atop state patrol cars in Arkansas.

"So," I said, after finishing the beer in my bottle, "you're having a baby?" This is what you call intuitive leapfrog.

SIX

I saw Dorothy Fleming's eyes in a restless dream. They changed to half dollars and then there were half dollars and shiny silver dollars everywhere I looked, tucked among the covers of her hotel bedding, piled loosely under the bed, tumbling out from behind her pillow. There were piles of glistening coins. I couldn't pick up all of them, but I tried to.

It was a thief's dream and, except for Dorothy Fleming, one I'd had before. The dream was as good as sex, though I always woke to a sharp feeling of loss, a numbing sadness. So maybe the dream was as bad as sex. My brooding discontent with reality upon waking had nothing to do with not actually having the coins in my possession. It was the joy I missed when in my dream I'd been so damn happy with finding a little money.

I'd grown up wanting it. I'd grown up poor in a small, broken town in Oklahoma. And, let me tell you, I wasn't the only guy in prison who believed in fairy tales in which straw is turned to gold.

I woke to the muffled sounds of the forced-air heat

coming on inside the house. Exhausted, I'd gone to bed before Avery had come in. I listened to Carolyn breathe in her sleep, her long back curved toward me, her knees tucked up.

I loved Carolyn in many ways. And I have to confess she was one of my favorite sexual fantasies, although I never fantasized about her in her presence. It was impossible to do. We knew each other too well. She'd know what I was thinking. It was only when I was alone and the fantasy was always as remote as living on a desert island.

But now I longed for her and she was lying next to me. This was no good for anybody. Our having sex would never work. We'd separately made that decision long ago, and neither so much as teased the other about the possibility. Or impossibility. You have sex with somebody, you may as well say good-bye while you're doing it. I counted on Carolyn being a part of my life. A part of my life I could always look up, could call from anywhere at any time, without feeling guilty about doing it.

Maybe I should go into the bathroom and shave. I could move slightly toward her, as if moving in my sleep, until I touched something, gently, warmly . . .

This was ridiculous. We knew each other far too well. We couldn't begin to make love without bursting into laughter. We couldn't even kiss. Still, she was there. She was warm, and suddenly I was afraid to move, afraid to breathe, lest Carolyn wake up to say something about my being clumsy.

Clumsy was a good word and it was exactly how I felt. I'd have smoked a cigarette if I'd had one. I deserved a cigarette. Perhaps I could locate one of Marilyn's downstairs. If nothing else, I could pilfer another Boulevard Pale Ale from the fridge. There was a round metal table on the deck by the pool. It seemed the perfect place to sit for a while and think things over.

Besides, it was my fatherly duty to check on Avery in the rumpus room.

Standing in the bedroom on the plush carpeting in my bare feet, I looked at my watch. It was a few minutes after midnight. I'd been dead to the world for hours. Nothing like an all-night drive to bring on a coma. Already wearing a T-shirt I'd worn to bed for Carolyn's sake, I slipped on my jeans over another pair of birthday boxer shorts and found my shoes.

Downstairs, I made my way through the oak-paneled dining room with the fancy chandelier and located the kitchen. The house was remarkably light and it took me a moment to figure it out. All the drapes were open, the curtains pulled back. Outside, a dozen security spotlights illuminated the dark acre of privacy circling the huge house.

Traipsing through someone else's house at night gives me the willies. Otherwise, I might have been a burglar instead of a car thief. I found myself tiptoeing into the rumpus room with my bottle of beer. Avery, or something approximating her form, was wadded up with a sleeping bag and several blankets on the folded-out sofa in front of Rowdy Monroe's unlit fireplace.

It was cool outside and I enjoyed the feel of the night air. I sat at the small metal table and watched the pool lights bubble up through the perfect blue-green water. Everyone in America should have a lighted swimming pool to gaze into at night. It was better than a lava lamp.

I pictured myself diving in, lying on the bottom and looking up. I wondered if you could see the stars at night from the bottom of a swimming pool. I wondered if you saw stars while lying in bed with a bullet hole in your forehead.

Tilting back the Boulevard, I was startled to see a figure standing atop the diving-board mount at the far end of the pool. It turned to look at me. I could see his face. It was asking me what the hell I was doing there and how long I expected to stay. It may have been the reflection of the lights off the water, but I could have sworn the figure's eyes were as big as fists. Baseballs.

Bringing down my beer, I got to my feet and walked purposefully to the end of the swimming pool. Nobody spoke. The man seemed to be wearing binoculars. He also appeared to be about ten feet tall. It wasn't until I was standing next to him, at the bottom of three metal steps at the mount end of the diving board, that Rowdy Monroe said hello.

"You must be Carolyn's friend," the major leaguer said.

"I'm Alton Franklin."

I reached up a hand and Rowdy shook it in a single grasp of fingers a classical pianist would die for. The binoculars turned out to be Rowdy's famous Coke-bottle glasses. He was barefoot, wearing white cotton slacks and a light-blue V-neck sweater. Mostly, he was huge. And lean. And tan.

He clambered down from the board, rotating a baseball in his left hand as if the red stitches were prayer beads and he were a full-time nun. I'd heard that a power pitcher's throwing arm was sometimes developed to twice the size of the other arm. It was a myth.

Rowdy Monroe was well balanced. Physically.

"I was peering over the back fence," he said almost shyly, embarrassed perhaps at having been caught. "You can see the Thirty-first Street broadcast tower from here. We're kind of on a hill."

It must have been a night for brooding. What I could see was the moon to the south, behind Rowdy. It looked like a brass doorknob you could reach up to and turn with one hand. Already smudged with fingerprints, the moon was best left alone. No telling how many dead women lay on the other, the dark side.

"Beyond that tower sometimes I think I can see Ness County at night. That's where I grew up."

"Way out on the windswept prairie," I said, half-joking.

"No shit about that. My dad's a rancher. Everybody else out there grows wheat and he about goes bust every year playing cowboy, ranging steers. I don't know why he does it. Thinks he's Wyatt Earp."

I was edgy. I don't enjoy hearing private revelations from near strangers. I consider it prying to read other people's horoscopes in the morning paper.

"I've been in about every state in this country, specially in the minors. Been about everywhere and you know what?"

"There's no place like home?" I tried not to patronize.

"That's about it. I love the emptiness I grew up in. I get claustrophobic in towns. You put me about anywhere they have hills or a lot of trees and I go nuts. Can't take it more than a day or two."

I wondered if he suffered claustrophobia in hotel rooms. I nodded solemnly, sipping the Boulevard.

"Think that's why I love baseball. You can be in the oldest, dirtiest city in America and, when you get out on that mound, it's like the sky opens up for you. It gets big again. And that field is big too, when you're standing in the middle of it."

"That must be the reason so many baseball players like golf."

Rowdy laughed at that. "Hate it," he said. "Can't fucking stand that game. It's the batters that like golf. They get to hit the ball every swing. It sits still for them."

I didn't have a thing to say about golf.

"I wouldn't mind living on a golf course," Rowdy admitted. "But I'd sure as hell plug up all those holes."

And throw up a barn or two, I thought. Stock the ponds, build a duck blind.

"You know some of those golf courses have quail on them?" he asked. "Quail living right there on the golf course."

Life was amazing. I entertained a picture of Rowdy Monroe in cowboy boots, hunting up quail with a nine iron. He'd probably bag a few.

"She's dead," I told the big farm kid standing next to me in the pool lights.

"I heard," Rowdy said without missing a beat. He looked down at me and blinked twice behind his thick lenses. I stared back, puzzled. I hadn't been certain he'd have the slightest idea what I was talking about.

"Heard it on the radio." Rowdy turned away. "Police didn't release the name pending notification of next-ofkin. But I knew it was her. Hell, I even knew the room number."

"How's that?"

"Oh, she sent a note to the clubhouse. Dorothy always does that once she gets her room."

"Along with a key?"

"Yeah," Rowdy mumbled. "She didn't know my brother was in town. He drove up for the weekend."

It was difficult to carry on an affair with the family loitering in town.

"Dead, damn, that's something," Rowdy said softly. "It's such a waste, you know? You're trying to get it all done somehow and then, just like that, you're dead."

There was nothing to say, which didn't seem to matter to Rowdy.

"I was out here wondering who would have done that," he confessed.

"Any ideas?"

"A few. Quite a few. There must be one or two players from every team. Minimum. Dorothy likes to . . ."

Not to mention their wives, I thought.

"Well, she *used* to raise a little hell."

"Was she blackmailing you?" I was thinking of the videotape.

"Hell no!" Rowdy roared, spinning on me, his jaw tightened in rage. I leaned back instinctively in case he threw a punch and watched while Rowdy's features softened a degree or two. "I think I love her," he said, talking to the open spaces on the other side of the fence.

Professional baseball players were rumored not to know a whole lot about the real world. Rowdy just proved it.

"I didn't find the car," I finally said.

"No luck, huh?"

"No luck."

"Well, thanks for looking. It was all pretty stupid. I threw a fit and scared Marilyn. She got carried away."

"You going to be able to pitch without the glove?"

Rowdy grinned. "I'll tell you what," he drawled, "I can toss ninety-five-mile-an-hour fastballs with an oven mitt on my other hand."

"But you had a bad outing?"

"I wasn't concentrating, that's all. Marilyn got it in her head I couldn't pitch without that old glove. It was my fault, really. I must have said something like that. I was upset the Caddy was stolen."

"From the driveway?"

"Pissed me off. Came right on my property and took the thing. It's the principle, you understand. I didn't really like the car. I bought a Caddy 'cause my dad always wanted one, you know. I was going to give it to him when I got my Porsche."

The principle? Maybe. Considering that Rowdy must know the videotape was in the trunk, I imagined he had a better reason for being upset. But I kept my mouth shut. If I told him I had the glove, he would know I also had the videotape. I'd as soon no one knew I'd even seen the damn thing.

Rowdy spun the baseball in his left hand, then brought it to a sudden stop with the squared-off fingernails of his first two fingers. "They're going to think I did it," he said. "The guys all know I was seeing her. They won't say anything, but someone might. Some guys tell their wives everything."

He sounded spooked.

"You were at the game when it happened," I said, offering Rowdy his alibi. And it was a good one.

"How did you know that? When was she killed?"

"It figures," I fumbled. "Uh, she sent the key to the clubhouse, so she was alive after you got there. And she was dead before the game was over."

"Is that what they said?" Rowdy seemed relieved. "I didn't know."

So far, only I had said she was dead before the game was over. It was an eerie feeling, but it seemed as if Rowdy knew that I was telling the truth.

Dorothy Fleming hadn't looked as if she'd been dead all day. Her already being dead would explain why Bird hightailed it, but it wouldn't explain how the videotape he was delivering ended up in her machine. I was fairly certain she'd been alive when Bird went to her room. Otherwise, he would have disappeared *with* the tape.

Rowdy placed a paw on my shoulder. I felt awkward, like being asked to dance with the ugliest girl in school. I'd felt this way in prison when other men got too close, even those innocent of intention.

"You think the police will want to talk to me?"

"Probably," I said, maneuvering out from under Rowdy's gesture of camaraderie. We began a slow walk toward the house.

"Hope this doesn't all come out like it did with Ray Twiggs. I mean, the guys won't say anything . . ." He trailed off. It seemed to be a rule of playing baseball that you kept your mouth eternally shut about other team members. It was probably a good rule. I played along with the rest of the guys and didn't say anything.

"Sammy can take care of it," the pitcher said rather loudly. "My agent. I pay him enough to take care of anything."

"Very funny," a new voice said, startling me. It came from the hot tub. It took me a moment of concentration to make out the shape of a head in the night shadows. There must have been a face on one side of it.

Everything we said had been overheard.

"Sammy Maxwell," Rowdy informed me, tossing the baseball into the tub. The head moved to one side quickly to let the ball plop into the water. "Attorney-at-law."

"Alton Franklin," I said to the lawyer in the hot tub. "Wrong side of the law." Nobody laughed.

"He's the guy Marilyn's sister brought along," Rowdy added.

"Nice to meet you," the voice said. "You're Avery's dad? Nice kid."

"If you say so."

"Sure she is. A real sweetheart."

Not that I trusted lawyers in the first place, but you had to question the honesty of anyone who claimed a thirteen-year-old terror to be a real sweetheart.

Rowdy touched me on the arm again. "I have an idea," he said, his voice looming above me. I waited to hear more while Rowdy inexplicably handed me his eyeglasses. Then Rowdy pulled his sweater over his head and discarded it on the bench. His arms wore the long, lean muscles of a horse's legs.

Rowdy took back his glasses and put them on. He stared at me for a long moment before speaking.

"Why don't you come out to the clubhouse tomorrow for batting practice? I can get you in, say that you're a writer or something. You can hang around the bull pen. Maybe pick up something."

"Bad idea," the lawyer said from shadow. Lawyers deserve to be despised.

"Pick up something?" I said. *Be on the field during a game!* Hey, I'd have picked up a trash bag of gum wrappers and dead bugs to be on the field during a game.

"Like who did it, who killed Dorothy."

"Bad idea," Rowdy's agent repeated.

"Her whole life was baseball, I can tell you that. It was somebody who had something to do with baseball. Maybe one of those Milwaukee guys. Maybe Billy Lee Burke can tell you something. He still lives in California, you know. He was staying at the Regal."

"Maybe the police already know who did it," I said.

"Sure," Rowdy scoffed, undoing his slacks. "And maybe the police could find my car. The guy on the radio said no leads, no suspects. Then they brought up all that horseshit about her and Ray Twiggs. That's old hat. He was out of her life for good."

Rowdy Monroe bent over to pull a pant leg free from one foot, then the other. He wasn't wearing underwear, not even a jockstrap. Casual nudity must be second nature to the big farm kid who'd spent half his life in locker rooms.

What bothered me wasn't Rowdy getting naked to take a hot tub. Rather, it was his casual confidence in me, as if anything a baseball player told another man wouldn't be shared with others.

"What do you say?" Rowdy asked, hands on his hips.

"Do you care who did it?"

"Very much."

"I strongly advise against it," the lawyer said. I wished I could see his face more clearly. The beer had gone right through me and his face might be something I'd want to piss on.

The police would either solve the murder or they wouldn't. In Kansas City, it was about fifty-fifty. And I still hadn't made up my mind whether Bird was capable of such a cold-blooded act. I doubted it, but the kid was weird. If he'd done it, Bird had made a big mistake.

I tapped the empty Boulevard bottle against my leg. Rowdy was waiting for an answer. It wasn't the murder I was considering, though it disturbed me. It was the chance to rub elbows with a couple dozen American heroes in full uniform. If Carolyn could make a vacation of the trip, there was no reason I shouldn't. I'd done my duty coming up with the baseball glove, not that anyone seemed to miss it all that much.

"You're on," I finally said.

SEVEN

I hadn't expected to like Rowdy Monroe.

For most of my life I'd resented athletes. I possessed a fair amount of physical stamina, but I'd never been adept at channeling my abilities within the requirements of a game. I have a negative reaction to anything that reeks of rules and regulations. My first fight, a one-sided affair, was the direct result of my lack of sports concentration.

Jimmy Brostin, a fourth-grade idiot who always captained one of the Phys Ed teams and who always picked me last when sides were chosen, punched me hard in the nose after school because I'd been daydreaming on first base during the inglorious period of the school day when fourth graders did their best to meet the physical requirements of our young and vigorous President.

The first rule of athletic competition: no daydreaming.

I was standing on the bag when Jimmy Brostin got a hit. And I was still standing there when he ran to first and was called out because it's a rule that two runners cannot occupy first base at the same time. Jimmy's face turned red with anger. He made promises he meant to keep.

Stunned by Jimmy's fist being slammed into my nose after school, I gave up on baseball. I held my fingers over my mouth and nose so no one could see the blood and walked slowly home from school. I considered taking up boxing. But that had rules too. Instead, I dropped by Jimmy Brostin's house that night and stole his bicycle from the front porch. It was never seen again.

The second rule of competition: hold a grudge long enough to get even.

The world rotated a few thousand times and, while young men were being paid huge sums for getting their butts off first and stealing second, I got hard time for getting caught stealing cars. Rules, rules, and more rules.

There might be a similar reason for Bird's having stolen Rowdy Monroe's Cadillac. It wasn't by accident that the fourteen-year-old made his way out to the fancy-pants suburbs to boost this particular car from this particular driveway in the middle of the morning. Maybe he knew that baseball players slept in on game days. Still, it would have made more sense for Bird to have waited until the Royals were on the road and Rowdy was safely out of town.

I lay atop the covers in my boxer shorts and my *Cordero Is My Guardian Angel* T-shirt. Carolyn's dark hair smelled lightly of lemon. It would have been easier to fall asleep if she'd been fat and ugly and smelled bad. Thankfully, I had major league baseball to think about to keep from dwelling on the possible details of the private reaches of the woman lying only inches away. Warm, easy inches.

I wanted to be on the turf at Royals Stadium tomorrow. I wanted to see Bo Jackson up close and in person. As I grew older, I no longer resented athletes. I marveled at their on-field accomplishments. With all-out grace they occasionally accomplished the impossible, hitting an unhittable pitch, catching an uncatchable ball. That desperate leap against the outfield wall to snag one on its way out of the park some days was the only truth left in America. It was something you could stand up and shout about.

I no longer resented athletes for their accomplishments, but I still had a hell of a time with rules.

When I woke, Carolyn's side of the bed was occupied, but not by Carolyn. Dorothy Fleming lay next to me.

Her eyes open, she looked as surprised as I was. I couldn't breathe. I couldn't turn my face away from her. I couldn't scream. A burglar alarm went off inside my head and I opened my eyes for real. Someone was in the room. Someone was standing at the foot of the bed staring at me.

"Are you two *doing it?*" Avery wanted to know. She wore a fourth of her brown hair dyed blue and sticking straight up. Avery had her mother's eyes and I always found that unsettling.

"That's none of your business."

"Carolyn'll tell me if you are, Dad. Carolyn tells me everything."

"I seriously doubt that. What are you doing up here?"

"Using the bathroom, what do you think?" She held her overnight case in one hand, her toothbrush in the other. "Unless you'd rather I barge in on Rowdy and

Marilyn. She's pregnant so they're probably not doing anything."

"Avery." It was our one-word code for her to shut up.

"But I read in *Cosmo* that some women don't experience orgasm until they're pregnant. In which case . . ."

"Avery?"

"Yeah, Dad."

"Who taught you to read?" I smiled. It almost worked.

"Well, I'll leave the shower on just in case."

"Wait a second. Let me in there before you get started." I got up and had my hand on the bathroom door when Avery said, "Da-aahd." She was going to ask for something.

"What?"

"Marilyn said I could get in the hot tub this morning. What do you think?"

"Don't drown," I said.

"I didn't bring a bathing suit."

"Wear a T-shirt and a pair of shorts."

"I'd look like a dweeb, dad!"

"So, borrow something."

"In case you haven't noticed, Carolyn and Marilyn are like double-C cups, Dad."

"So wear a T-shirt and a pair of shorts."

"What I mean is, you know, people get into hot tubs without any clothes on. It's like taking a bath."

"Not thirteen-year-old people," I said. "Wear a T-shirt and shorts."

"I could wrap up in a towel, and wrap it back on as soon as I get—"

"No."

74

"You always treat me like I'm a baby," Avery charged, her voice breaking. Thirteen-year-olds favor melodrama.

"Maybe if you wouldn't act like one . . ."

"Avery," Carolyn said, propping up in bed, "the men will be going to the ballpark today." How did she know? "Rowdy's getting them on the field for batting practice. We'll have a couple hours before we go and you can get in the hot tub then."

"Nude?" Avery asked me, finding in it all the romance a one-syllable word could hold.

"Okay," I relented. "But wear a towel to and from."

"You never know when a helicopter might be in the neighborhood," Carolyn said.

I didn't like the world Avery was being brought up in. There was too much information on TV. Too much information in Danielle Steel books, Avery's favorite reading material. But I was a father and an official dweeb, what did I know?

While I was using the facilities, Carolyn slipped on a light sundress with shoestring straps.

"I'd appreciate it if you wouldn't take sides," I told her once I heard the shower come on.

"Don't be silly. She's the only child in the house, Alton, and she can use a friend." Carolyn brushed her hair in the dresser mirror.

"It's difficult enough—"

"I'm going downstairs to help with breakfast," Carolyn said, cutting me off. "I took my shower last night." That's why she smelled so good, I thought.

"Besides, I'm going to be in the bull pen during the game," I said to the bedroom door she closed quietly be-

75

hind her. "Anybody can get on the field during batting practice."

I needed coffee. It was doubtful anyone would bring it up to me, so I dressed and made my way downstairs. I needed to talk to Carolyn about when we'd leave Kansas City. Five minutes after today's game, if I had my way, which rarely happened when either Avery or Carolyn was involved.

I was thinking that maybe I should tell Carolyn everything—about the glove, the tape, the murder—when I discovered Marilyn in the kitchen doing something with her hands. Dressed in her white bathrobe with pink piping, she made juice from orange halves, her back to me. As she worked, the cloth of the robe outlined the delicious shapes of those perfect halves.

I knew what she'd worn under her robe last night and I didn't want to think about that. Things were hard enough around here. Marilyn's right elbow lifted and fell as she twisted the fruit down on the reamer. I could smell everything too strongly.

I couldn't think of anything to say. Eventually, she noticed me. Marilyn Monroe turned and smiled. She had one of those perfect haircuts, just above the shoulders, that settle into place with a flick of her head.

"Rowdy won't be up for an hour. He hates early-game days. And this will be two in a row. During the season, he usually sleeps till noon."

I felt as if I were on a tour of Graceland and the King himself was still alive, sleeping one off upstairs.

"I really can't thank you enough for looking for Rowdy's car. That was so sweet of you."

Sure, it was. And I'd left the dead woman lying there with her eyes open. Real sweet. But what the hell, I had her on tape. Alive . . . and kicking.

Marilyn was smiling again. People she knew didn't have bullet holes in their heads. I wanted to tell Marilyn I had a videotape of her upstairs Elvis fucking a dead woman and ask her what *her* intentions were.

Why was I feeling such animosity? Marilyn turned from me and, while pouring fresh-squeezed from the reamer into a glass, kept talking.

"I know Rowdy will pretend otherwise, but that old glove is very important to him. I thought he was going to tear down the house. It even took me by surprise."

It goes like this. You find a dead woman. You meet your best friend's sister. You want to climb all over her goodies with your tongue hanging out. Then you're angry as hell at her for being in the kitchen in the first place.

"I didn't think you could find it, but Carolyn was so insistent. She's really hung up on you." Sisters! "Anyway, it was worth a shot. Rowdy would want to know that all avenues have been exhausted."

She wiped her hands on a kitchen towel as if to say *So much for that.*

"Coffee?" I said, having to clear my throat to speak.

Marilyn held out a hand to me. "This way. I'll introduce you."

She led me by the hand through, down, and out onto the redwood deck, where Carolyn sat at the metal table with a curly-haired man wearing a red T-shirt eighteen sizes too small for him. Two empty coffee cups were stacked on the table next to a china pot overlooking a plate of croissants.

The sun had topped the fence and the May morning felt as warm as July. Carolyn's hair was wet and she wore a towel over her shoulders like a shawl. Her legs were bare. She'd been in the pool. I caught a glimpse of an edge of her yellow one-piece swimsuit. Her sundress was draped over the back of an empty chair.

"This is Reno Stouth," Marilyn said, releasing my hand, which now smelled pleasantly of oranges.

Reno stood to shake hands across the table. The guy was an electrically-tanned ape with perfect teeth. Though not as tall, he outweighed me by sixty pounds, and none of it was anything but muscle. His red T-shirt was stenciled *Body by Reno.* Nobody could blame his mother for having created it. A tree-trunk neck, the rest of Reno Stouth's muscular torso was a walking testament to the power of steroids abuse. His grasp nearly crushed my fingers, which was, I figured, the idea. The wrong person had been pulping oranges.

"He's Rowdy's personal trainer," Marilyn said.

Small dick, I told myself. Reno released my hand and I used it to rub a kink in the back of my neck.

"And this is Alton Franklin. He was looking for Rowdy's car."

"Some girl you got there," Reno said, pushing back his metal deck chair to sit down again. He sat slowly. On purpose, I guessed, so everyone could enjoy watching his thighs flex. Bodybuilders bore me. Hell, they bore everybody. Except themselves.

Small dick, I told myself again. This guy had better keep an eye on his bicycle.

Carolyn grinned at me maniacally, in case I'd missed the point that she was the "some girl" Reno referred to. Marilyn poured a cup of coffee for me.

"Yes, isn't she." I patted Carolyn on the head. I'd pay for it sometime later, but I couldn't resist the urge. "Very devoted," I added. "Been following me around for years."

I took a sip of coffee and my head began to clear. "Waxes the car, chops wood, mends fences." I kept going. "Why, did you know she'll swim right out in the river to fetch a ball when you throw it—"

"What river?" Marilyn asked, her questioning expression on sideways as she sat in the chair with Carolyn's sundress draped over the back. Clearly, she feared for her sister's safety.

Without looking at me, Carolyn lifted the middle finger of her right hand and pointed it in my direction.

But Reno laughed good-naturedly. So he wasn't all that stupid. Long, thick things that had once been normal muscle tissue danced under Reno's red shirt as he laughed. The guy was like the elephant in a circus. You wanted to reach out and touch him to see for yourself if he were real. Balls the size of peanuts, I bet.

"Hi, Dad!" Avery called from somewhere. Still standing, I lifted my coffee cup to her after finding her perched on the end of the diving board, wearing a soaked T-shirt and a pair of wet shorts. Mark one up for fathers everywhere.

There were heads in the hot tub.

"How's it going?" one of the heads said in a particularly disinterested way when my gaze drifted in that direction.

"That's Richard, Rowdy's brother," Marilyn said. "And Gary and Sandra and Julie. Richard's friends from college." One of the girls said hello. At least I knew what the other bedrooms were being used for.

"Richard just worships his brother," Marilyn said in a low, conspiratorial voice. She made it sound somehow as if she didn't. "He's always driving people up to meet Rowdy." Marilyn withdrew a package of menthol cigarettes and a plastic lighter from a pocket of her bathrobe. She poured herself the last cup of coffee.

"Sammy should be showing up soon," Marilyn added once she had a smoke going. "Rowdy's agent. They're inseparable. You'd think he bought this house. Practically lives here."

"We met last night," I admitted. Not that I got a look at his face.

"You want to get wet?" Carolyn asked me. It sounded like a threat.

"Maybe later."

"I don't swim," Reno chimed in. "But it's good for building up the wind." Reno looked as if he could cut a mean stroke through drying cement.

"You run instead?" I asked.

"Yeah."

"Through brick walls?"

Reno laughed. He seemed to like me.

"What you got is a Yankee smart mouth," he said. "My brother's like that. You just never know what he's going to say next."

That was it all right, a Yankee smart mouth. You learn it from your mother when she was born in Louisiana and never got farther north than Oklahoma.

"Treadmill," Reno said when no one else found anything to say. "I run on a treadmill. Water and me don't mix. When I was five I walked off a diving board. They had to bring me up from the bottom. I sat there. On the bottom." He looked from face to face to see who was listening. "Haven't been back since."

"Has anyone seen the paper?" I asked.

"I forgot to grab it," Marilyn said. "It's probably out front. If you'd like . . ."

I sat my empty coffee cup on the table and walked back toward the house. At my back I heard Avery yelp as she finally forced herself off the diving board. Despite my confidence in her ability to float, I turned to watch. She came to the surface and swam noisily to the nearest side. Whatever she put on the blue portion of her hair had it sticking up like a fin.

Finding the paper, even the Sunday *Star*, was like an Easter egg hunt on the Monroes' front lawn. Rowdy's father could fatten a few calves on this pasture. I eventually located it on the other side of the driveway, taking note of the cars. There was a Volvo station wagon. Marilyn's. And there was a four-wheel-drive Jeep with a *WSU Wheatshockers* bumper sticker. Richard's. Or Gary's. Or Sandra's or Julie's.

My van was at the distant curb, holding evidence. I was still considering telling Carolyn everything. She deserved to know. The tape, the glove, the murder. It was *her* family. What are friends for?

The murder was on the second page of the Metropolitan section, which was tucked between the black-and-white bra and panties ads, a regular highlight of the KC paper. The brief article identified Dorothy Fleming as having been shot to death in her hotel room. The newspaper left out the name of the hotel.

A spokesman for the Major Cases Squad of the KCMO police was quoted as saying robbery appeared to be the motive behind the killing of this minor celebrity. What was it Marilyn had said? *A good deal of life has nothing to do with reality.* Apparently, so did a good deal of death.

The reporter hadn't wondered in print why Dorothy Fleming was in town. He did note that her purse and jewelry had been taken, according to the police report.

"Not so," I muttered. Not until after I'd left Room 931.

There was a short rundown of Miss Fleming's career in the public spotlight, including the fact that she'd appeared in the buff in a major men's magazine.

The paper did not leave out the name of the magazine.

Kansas City had recently breezed into the top ten American cities in number of homicides per year. Some were investigated more thoroughly than others. The KCMO police might blame this one on the Fairy Gun Mother. The murder hadn't warranted enough column inches of ink to rate a full-scale investigation.

Of course, the police didn't know that simple robbery wasn't the motive.

I skimmed the remainder of the paper. What a town. Illegal gambling flourished on both sides of the state line. There was the usual prostitution and crack cocaine arrests. Jamaican and LA street gangs had established beachheads in the city. Local politicians routinely forgot to pay their taxes. A county legislator convicted of bribery had petitioned a district judge to reduce his five-year sentence to Leavenworth so he could be released now. Having served all of three months, the former legislator had discovered that being in the federal pen was disrupting his family life.

I wondered what the hell a county legislator does. Go to jail seemed the obvious answer.

Kansas City didn't appear to be making the world a better place for anybody. Forget the Bible Belt; this town was walking around with its pants unzipped.

I got pissed. The damn paper left out everything. It reported a murder, but the murder wasn't there. The newspaper overlooked death in its report of Dorothy Fleming's killing. It left out a mention of the sudden process that reduced a lifetime of accumulated learning and feeling to a few gray pounds of immobile gore.

It left out just how the total of a person's dreams and memories, aspirations and accomplishments, her future and past, escaped in one flush moment through a smokehole blasted into Dorothy Fleming's skull. The paper left out that her eyes were open. The paper omitted what she did and did not see.

And it left out the fact there were children in backyards, in swimming pools and on swing sets, children in wet T-shirts perched on diving boards, children whose entire lives were wasted if we allowed lives to end like this. That was murder.

EIGHT

I returned to the deck with the paper under my arm. Marilyn said something about saving the sports section for Rowdy, retrieved it from the large lump of newsprint I'd discarded on the tabletop, and carried it to the sliding glass doors, then disappeared inside the huge house.

Reno Stouth read my mood and without saying anything dug through the sections for something to look at. Voices lifting from the hot tub sounded like people talking in their sleep.

Avery was stretched out on her back on the diving board. She'd rolled up her soaked T-shirt so her belly could take the morning sun. What's a vacation without a tan? I don't know why, but I was saddened by the picture. I loved her. I regretted what she'd be going through in order to grow up.

I'd have taken her then to buy a swimsuit, but I could think of no single store that sold bathing suits that was open on Sunday morning. Unless 7-Elevens were carrying them now. Next, I'd be refusing to buy things in

Styrofoam containers so the universe would be a better place for her.

"We need to talk," I said to Carolyn. Her hair was nearly dry. It should be safe.

Reno started to get up. "That's okay," I told him.

I touched Carolyn on the arm and suggested we go for a walk. I didn't want to talk in the house. It seemed to be listening. I snatched a croissant. Carolyn wrapped herself in her towel and we ended up out front, strolling toward the van.

I took the driver's seat. She climbed in the passenger side.

"The grass felt good," she chirped merrily. "First time I've been barefoot this year."

"Things aren't as wonderful as they seem."

"Gawd, Alton, I know that. Rowdy's been screwing around. And Marilyn's having an affair, I'm almost certain. They're not a happy couple. Nobody should be pregnant when a marriage isn't working. And no one should get pregnant while she's having an affair. Do you know how many days a year Rowdy's out of town?"

"I found the glove, Carolyn."

I started the van and turned the air conditioner on so we could keep the windows up.

"I thought you said you didn't." She wrapped the towel more tightly around her shoulders. "Are you trying to give me goose bumps?"

"It's a thought." I turned the air conditioner on low. "I said I didn't find the car. I found the glove, though. That kid I was telling you about? Bird. He had it. He stole Rowdy's car Friday morning and took the glove out of the trunk."

"Why didn't you give it to Rowdy? Does this, uh, Bird still have it?"

"Someone's been murdered," I said, watching a small red sports car pull into the Monroe driveway.

"Alton! Don't tease me."

"Seriously. It was Rowdy's girlfriend. It was in the paper this morning. I saw the body."

"You saw the body?" She was staring at me wide-eyed, the towel off her shoulders now.

"In her hotel room. The paper said the police think it was robbery. I don't think so."

"You were in her hotel room?"

"It's a long story. The reason I didn't mention the glove is there was something else in the trunk of Rowdy's Cadillac. A videotape that, as it turns out, is rather incriminating."

The sports car parked. A man in a suit hopped out. He was small. His hurried walk looked familiar. I'd seen him before. "Who is that? Do you know?"

"Might be Rowdy's agent, that Maxwell guy," Carolyn said. It was also the man I'd seen rushing along the ninth-floor corridor of the Regal Inn yesterday. I hadn't recognized him sitting in the hot tub last night and now I wondered if he'd recognized me. Sammy Maxwell went into the house.

"Did you call the police?" Carolyn wanted to know.

I rolled my eyes in reply. "I couldn't tell anyone I had the glove because the video is of Rowdy and his girl-friend having sex in a hotel room. If he knew I'd found the glove, he'd know I had the tape."

"Do you?"

"Yes. That's why I went up to her room. Bird was

supposed to be selling her the tape. I thought I'd talked him into dropping it off. When he didn't come out, I went in. The tape was in a VCR in her hotel room. She was dead, Carolyn. I took it back and got the hell out of there."

"Who killed her?" Carolyn's voice was shaky.

"Who cares?"

"You . . . don't think it was Rowdy?"

"No. I think she was killed during the game. In fact, I'm sure of it."

"He didn't pitch, Alton."

"Relievers are in the bull pen. Thousands of people had to see him sitting out there."

"That's a relief." She pulled the towel up, holding it closed at the front of her neck.

"I suppose."

"What? You think he knows who did it? You think he paid somebody to do it?"

"He asked me last night if I could find out who killed her. He wants me to ask around."

"Tell him to screw himself," Carolyn spat. "Who was it? What's her name?"

"Dorothy Fleming. The baseball groupie. She was all over the news for a while back with the Ray Twiggs scandal, suing for support because he'd damaged her career by asking her to travel wherever the team went during the season."

"Strangled? Beat up? Gawd, Alton, what?"

"Shot. Once in the forehead, close range, with a small handgun."

"Did he have a gun? This kid, did he have a gun?"

"I think so. He said he did."

"So they fought about the tape. She didn't want to pay him and he shot her. Bird shot her. Call the police and turn him in anonymously."

"But the tape was still there, Carolyn. I have it now. If he'd shot her, Bird would have taken the tape."

She thought about it. "At least I know why you couldn't sleep last night. Was it awful seeing her body?"

What could I say?

Carolyn propped her chin forward and tried to smile. "Well, I guess that's the end of this vacation," she said.

"Uh, I was thinking of going to the game."

"Not a good idea, Alton. We ought to pack our bags, say good-bye, and leave. But before we do, you have to call the police and tell them about this Bird character. Even if he didn't kill her, he was there."

"And they'll find out I was there. I can't do it, Carolyn."

"Yes, you can."

"I have Avery to think about."

"What's his name? You know his name?"

"Yes."

"So give it to me and I'll call the cops. I'll call them from a filling station in St. Louis. They'll pick him up and it will all be over."

I started to convince her otherwise when I was interrupted by a noise in the back of the van. Bird came forward in a crouch from his hiding place. I saw him in the rearview mirror. He'd heard everything.

"I'll tell them it was you," Bird said loudly. He sounded afraid. "I'll tell them it was you, Rooster. I'll say you bragged about it."

"I'm not turning you in, kid. And neither is she."

Carolyn turned in her seat.

"I didn't do it, Rooster. She was dead when I got there." Bird sounded as if he were about to cry.

Carolyn stared at the hunched-over kid in the red leather jacket. Bird started to say something, but when she saw his small chrome-colored handgun she screamed. I hadn't thought he would use it until then. Screams tend to make people holding guns nervous.

Bird cursed, dove sideways and slid open the side-door of the van before I could think to lock the doors. It was just as well. No sense locking yourself and a woman you love inside a van with a nervous kid holding a loaded gun.

Bird trotted down the street.

"Get him," Carolyn urged. The towel had slipped entirely off her shoulders. A strap of her bathing suit was down. "Alton!" She glanced at me and then out the window at Bird's escape. "Catch that son of a bitch!" He ran down the middle of the road and I wondered where, if anywhere, Bird had to go. We were a long way from his neighborhood.

"I don't think he did it," I said calmly.

"I don't give a crap. That juvenile delinquent pointed a gun at me. Run over his ass!"

A woman with wet hair, I'm telling you, is like betting two-year-old fillies in the rain.

NINE

Turning off the engine, I removed the key from the ignition switch as Bird turned the corner a long block ahead
of us. Maybe he wanted me to catch him. But I had family in the house. Carolyn tramped across the Monroe
lawn. I watched her go inside. She'd left behind her
towel and the smell of chlorine.

I couldn't decide whether we'd caught Bird in the act
or he had been waiting to talk to me. Either way, it was
worth checking and I unlocked the small cabinet beneath
the fold-out bench-bed in the back of the van. Rowdy's
missing glove cradled the videotape from Dorothy Fleming's hotel room.

Also in place was my .32 automatic, fully loaded, and a
plain white envelope that held forty-two crisp C-notes. It
was my betting pool. You never know when you might
come across a racetrack. Every state in our illustrious
union seems to have recently passed pari-mutuel wager-
ing legislation. Woodlands, the Kansas City, Kansas,
track was running dogs at the moment.

Unlike thoroughbreds, greyhounds didn't race. They

simply gave chase. The only bet I could figure at a dog-track was to back the mechanical rabbit.

Carolyn needed time to calm down. I decided to talk to Avery. She'd been at the game yesterday.

I locked the van for the hell of it. The only way to keep a practiced car thief out of a vehicle was to wrap it in chains. Even that would prove to be nothing more than a delay. Bird hadn't wanted the van or it would have been gone. He'd wanted to talk to me. Or he'd wanted the tape.

I hiked the small piece of prairie encircling the house to discover everyone was missing at poolside. The hot tub was empty and had been turned off. There was a croissant left on the table, along with the cups and the coffeepot.

Some vacation, I thought. Everyone had a good time yesterday but me and Dorothy Fleming. I never should have found that glove. I should have gone to the ballpark instead. I should have eaten nachos and hot dogs, read the scoreboard, spilled beer and watched Bo Jackson strike out. I should have sat there like everyone else with my heart's fingers crossed for the occasional miracle that brings tens of thousands of people simultaneously to their feet to applaud.

I righted a metal deck chair that had been toppled and sat down for my second go at breakfast. The croissant had turned stale in the sun and the coffee was barely warm. Where had everyone gone? It was as if eight people suddenly and at the same time decided to take a quick raspberry douche.

Sammy Maxwell had been to Dorothy Fleming's hotel room and that troubled me. I suspected the small, red-faced overdresser had been the one who'd taken her purse and jewelry. A false motive gets everyone off the hook. He'd set up the robbery to protect someone and I was wondering if that someone might not be himself.

Had Bird, or someone else altogether, killed her, Maxwell would no doubt still have been inclined to set up the faux robbery to keep his star client from being drawn into the mess. Bad guys. Good guys. Go figure.

I eyed the fence that Rowdy was so fond of looking over whenever he learned a girlfriend had been murdered. You could see all the way to his father's cattle ranch in the middle of Kansas by gazing over that fence. You could see into the future and the past. You bet.

If I'd seen Maxwell in the ninth-floor hallway, he'd seen me. And he'd had all night to think about it.

Right now a spring starling was holding down the fort, perched on Rowdy and Marilyn's redwood fence. Its yellow eyes studied the surface of the swimming pool. All that water and not one drop of it to drink.

There was something floating in the pool, in the near corner. I had to stand up to get a look at it. The object appeared at first to be a basketball with wet hair. I walked closer, staring, more curious than alarmed.

When I was close enough, the basketball turned into a human head. There was a massive red-shirted body attached. Reno Stouth had taken a dive, a different kind of dunk shot.

Leaping into the pool feet first, I sank nearly to the bottom then bobbed back up. The water was cold and it stung my eyes. I dog-paddled, pushing the body toward the shallow end. Though heavy, it seemed to be full of air and moved right along.

Reno's skin was blue. It was too late. His eyes were closed. A red and purple bruise darkened his temple, where his head must have hit the pool's concrete edge when he slipped. Rim shot. Treading water, gulping for breath, I pushed Reno's unsinkable tonnage back. Just like real life to do this to me. There was no shallow end.

I yelled for help.

TEN

We gathered in the rumpus room at Sammy Maxwell's request.

Avery was upstairs, along with the college girls, Sandra and Julie. Carolyn sat on the couch in front of the fireplace, Richard's dumpy college pal next to her. Gary was short and round. He breathed heavily with his mouth open under dark slits for eyes. His face looked like he shaved with a spatula and his haircut was in worse shape.

Gary must be Richard's creature, I thought, the hanger-on, the odd roommate everyone got when they moved into the dorm. Or into a prison cell. He probably wrote Richard's papers for him. Gary had tried to speak to Carolyn about Nicaragua, but she was having none of it.

Richard was the golden boy, slumped in a leather chair under Rowdy's enlarged baseball card. He looked lean, strong, handsome and bored. He pitched on the Wichita State team, which was as good as the minors and probably more fun. Like his brother, Richard was a hurler; but, unlike Rowdy, he threw right-handed.

The King of Slick leaned against the pool table, his arms crossed, ready to orate. Sammy Maxwell wore a piece of silk that matched his tie in the pocket of his tailored suit jacket, a gold watch that would cost most Americans a twenty-year mortgage, and a smirk that meant business.

I stood in the doorway, near one of Rowdy's weight machines, looking damn silly. My hair was wet. My soaked-through jeans squeaked when I walked. I wore a towel in place of a shirt and my socks had been left with my shoes on the redwood deck. Carolyn couldn't look at me and keep from laughing. Among other things, I was thinking that everything in my wallet had been ruined.

We were waiting for Marilyn to return. She'd found time to disappear into the kitchen, but I suspected she'd dashed upstairs to have a word with Rowdy. He was being kept at a safe distance from everything.

"All right," Sammy said, loosening his arms to tug the brilliant white cuffs of his shirt into view under the honed edges of his jacket sleeves. Four buttons each. "The girls are upstairs. They were there the whole time. We won't have them come down at all."

"They didn't see anything," Richard said, dealing with facts.

"And they didn't hear anything," Sammy added. "They've got nothing to say to anyone."

"Right," Richard said as if his jaw ached.

I heard a click in the other room. Marilyn finally returned, sliding by me with a drink in her hand. A good idea, a drink. I held up my hand to stop Sammy from talking and darted out the doorway before Rowdy's business manager could protest.

She'd been on the phone. I'd heard her hang up. I found it in the sitting room where I'd been introduced to Marilyn the night before. The plastic phone was on the small table at the end of the flowered sofa. I snatched up the receiver and did my trick. This time I hit the payoff.

"Jim," a voice answered, a voice I'd heard before.

I hung up and hurried into the kitchen, my bare feet cold on the tile floor. I cornered a Boulevard Pale Ale, opened it and made my way back to the doorway of the rumpus room. Everything smelled like chlorine now, including the beer.

"Thank you," Sammy said sarcastically upon my reunion with the gang. I bowed.

Sammy Maxwell's eyes were dark brown, almost black. They were intense eyes, eyes that took in information and gave nothing away.

"This is how it goes," he announced, holding up both hands. Napoleon's own remake of Waterloo. "Rowdy and I left for the ball game. The girls are upstairs. Marilyn's in the kitchen, fixing something. What?"

"Juice," Marilyn said, letting everyone in the room know she despised the small man in the silk tie. Truly beautiful women can do that with one word. They learn how in the first grade when they say *"Thanks"* to some kid like me for giving them all his crayons.

"Okay then, juice." Sammy paused. "You," he said, pointing at Carolyn and snapping his fingers twice.

"Carolyn," I said for him.

"Right. Carolyn, you're upstairs too. Blow-drying your hair. Everyone else just had breakfast and you were changing into clothes, you know, maybe a quick shower, something like that. I'll leave it up to you. But as soon as we're through here, you go do it."

"Should she take off what she's wearing and put her wet bathing suit back on, *then* take it off and get in the shower?" Marilyn sniped.

"The idea," Sammy countered, "is to tell the truth."

I kept from laughing by sucking beer down my throat.

"Reno slipped, fell, hit his head," Sammy went on. "Splash! An accident. It happens. We have to let whoever shows up to ask the questions figure it out for themselves. Nobody here saw anything, and that's the truth."

I wondered.

"You." Sammy pointed at Gary without waiting to be reminded of his name. "You're watching the tube. You don't see anything. Turn it on and look at what's on as soon as we leave. And that's what you'll say you were watching when Richard yells. Then you go out on the deck to help him get Reno out of the pool."

Gary nodded, ready for any assignment.

"And that's when you call 911, Marilyn. Say there's been an accident. That's true. Give them your name and address, ask for an ambulance, and hang up. They'll try to keep you on, but just hang up. You're upset. Got it?"

"That's also true," Marilyn said, as much to herself as to anyone in the room.

"Then call me at the ballpark," Sammy continued. "The front office. Have me paged. I'll get somebody to come out here to handle the police. Rowdy's pitching today—nobody gets to him. I'll tell him about Reno after the game. That's the story. That's the way it happens."

"Okay, Richard. I want you to go out there and roll

Reno back into the pool. As soon as we're gone. No, give us five minutes. Then yell at him"—Sammy pointed at Gary once more—"and jump into the pool with your clothes on."

Richard was ready for his role, but he didn't seem avid about it. I took another pull from my beer. For a guy who didn't know how to swim, Reno was sure ending up in the water a lot. If it had been a suicide, his T-shirt, *Body by Reno*, would have meant something.

"Do I go outside?" Gary asked, sounding anxious.

"Right. Leave the TV on, run out there and help Richard get the body out of the pool. Jump in if you have to."

I eyed the trophy shelves. Among the artifacts of Rowdy's athletic career were about thirty small wooden pedestals, upon which signed baseballs were perched. Some of the baseballs were bruised, smudged, while others were like new. There was one empty pedestal on the end, waiting for Rowdy's next important strikeout.

"What was I doing out there?" Richard asked.

"Nothing," Sammy said. "It's Sunday morning. You'd just come from changing upstairs to, uh, check on your pal here. You know, see what your houseguest was up to. And you walk outside to see if the hot tub was turned off. Maybe you forgot to do it. Leave the glass doors open. You see Reno's body and yell. Jump in. And that's it."

"Got it," Richard said with a remarkable sense of ennui.

"Okay, folks, just like it actually happened. Only Rowdy's not here. Reno's out there by himself. Just like it happened. There are no witnesses. You don't know how he got into the pool. Nobody saw anything."

That bird on the fence, I thought, saw it all. Carolyn

was right. We ought to get the hell out of here. I was thankful Avery had been upstairs in our room. The only window opened onto the front lawn. I wondered if she'd seen Bird tumble out of the van and run down the street.

"Any questions?"

I lifted my hand like a student. "I've got one."

"Rowdy wants you at the game. That means you leave with us. You have a criminal record, I understand. We don't want you to have discovered the body. It might make the papers. You, me, and Rowdy have left for the game. And that's going to happen right now."

"Uh, I mean I had a question," I said.

Sammy raised his eyebrows and waited, his dark eyes empty. Everyone, including Richard, turned to look at me.

"Who's Jim?" I said.

No one answered.

No one seemed to care.

"Is that it?" Sammy wanted to know.

"Not at all," I said, deciding to enter the conversation and alter Sammy's best-laid plans to my liking. "My daughter, she's with me. Or I stay here."

"Yeah?" Sammy thought about a second. "Fine. She'll go to the ballpark with us. What's her name?"

"Carolyn too," I added. "If she wants to come along."

"I'd rather stay with Marilyn, I think," Carolyn told me, her blue eyes clear with her intent.

"Now!" Sammy said to everyone, clapping his hands. "I'm upstairs to get Rowdy. Then we're out of here." He turned to me. "You're outside by the car. Get dressed, for God's sake. Okay, let's go, everybody!"

Carolyn caught my eye before I turned to leave the room. *Who's Jim?* she mouthed silently. Wish I knew. Marilyn hadn't batted an eye when I'd asked the question.

ELEVEN

It was time to root root root for the home team. Rowdy did the honors, driving his agent's sports car. Avery was delighted to make the early trip to Royals Stadium a foursome even though it meant cramming into the tiny backseat with her father.

"Sorry to leave so early," Rowdy said to the rearview mirror. "I need to do some work on the legs. Reno was going to help me at the house, but . . ."

"He'll use the machines in the training room," Sammy filled in the backseat tourists. I had to sit with my head tucked slightly forward.

"So, Franklin, you still on the case for me?" Rowdy asked, as if discussing the weather or the traffic instead of a lover's death.

"I'll keep my ears open," I promised.

"What case?"

"Finding out who stole his car," Sammy said before Rowdy could glibly tell all. "You're going to be a writer," he added, turning in his seat to look obliquely into the rear reaches of the car's interior. "Someone nobody would know. Say that you're doing a piece for an in-flight magazine, how's that?"

This was Sammy's world and welcome to it, I thought. He put a writer in the bull pen, the poor people in the ghetto. Rich people had private swimming pools. Poor kids got the shitty schools. Gorgeous women married athletes. And, let's see, baseball groupies all stayed in the same hotel.

"Should I have a notebook or something?"

"Hell no," Rowdy said, downshifting. "Writers hang around for a day and make up what they want to. You start taking notes, people will think you're a scout for another team and you'll get kicked out of the pen."

"Are you really going to write an article, Dad?"

I patted Avery's leg, the knee of which was impaling my thigh, as if to answer her question. Finally, I pushed against it, but her leg didn't budge. In turn, she poked me in the ribs with her elbow and stuck out her tongue at me. The blue streak in her hair looked like an ostrich feather.

We drove by a billboard that proclaimed Kansas City to be the "Used-Carpet Capital of the World." Bet the Chamber of Commerce loved this one. I pictured a city of bald men wearing previously owned toupees. Then the Truman Sports Complex popped into view. Arrowhead Stadium, home of the Chiefs and the occasional off-season mudathon, loomed deep and wide behind Royals Stadium with its scoreboard shaped like a crown.

Sammy removed an M-lot parking slip from the glove compartment and hung it over the post of the rearview mirror.

"I'm going in today," Rowdy told his agent. "I can feel it."

"You bet you are," Sammy said.

"I'm never wrong, you know?" Rowdy announced to the backseat. "It's like the stadium gives off an electrical charge. I always know when I'm going to pitch."

"Really?" Avery said, fascinated.

How odd a world it was for a thirteen-year-old, I thought. In Avery's world, Randall Monroe was a handsome guy who made a lot of money staying tan. It was as if he'd simply been non-dweeb and ungeek enough to ask to do it. Her father, on the other hand, wasn't smart enough to ask to be on a team. He didn't look the part. They'd never let her father pitch in the majors.

In Avery's world, Reno was just now slipping on the deck, nose-diving into the pool and banging his head on its hard edge. She'd find out about it when the others showed up for the game. And I had no doubt they'd all be there.

Upstairs, I'd asked Avery about yesterday's game. Apparently she hadn't stayed in her seat long enough to know whether everyone else did. Sammy, she'd remembered, hadn't sat with them at all. And Marilyn had left to say hello to people in the enclosed suites upstairs. Richard and Gary talked after the game about having gone into the sportscasters' booths, but Avery hadn't been there at the time. She'd been "you know, Dad, walking around to see the guys and stuff. They dress just like back home. There was this awesome guy with three earrings in one ear. He was with a girl wearing this awful . . ." Avery had concluded with, "A lot of fat people go to ball games, Dad."

M-lot, a small, virtually enclosed parking area on the south side of the stadium, was nearly full. Many of the expensive cars had personalized tags. Bird could make a killing here. It was anybody's guess what the other ballplayers stowed in their trunks and glove compartments.

Rowdy was on edge by the time we piled out of the little red car. He disappeared without looking back, on his way to the locker room. Sammy led me and Avery into the front offices that doubled as a poster gallery of Royals in action. I'd almost forgotten Freddy Patek, but there he was in large four-color, suspended horizontally between second and third to snag a line drive.

Sammy flirted with the receptionist, snatching a half-dozen official Royals baseballs from an open carton behind her desk. "Put it on my account," he said, winking. She handed him a Royals gym bag, which Sammy handed in turn to Avery.

"Autographs," the agent told my daughter. "Stand around the outfield side of the dugout. They'll come over. You have a pen?"

Avery played it cool. She wasn't sure she was interested in autographs.

"Maggie?" Sammy held out his hand.

The receptionist came up with a blue felt-tip.

"George Brett's still single, you're interested in millionaires," Sammy told Avery as he passed along the pen.

Avery couldn't take much more and turned to me with her eyes crossed. I fished two damp twenties from my front pocket and forked them over. Hot dogs and soda pop. Autonomy.

"Two rows back, home dugout," Sammy said, giving Avery her ticket, which she crammed into the back pocket of her jeans along with the forty bucks. "What you need to do, darling, is go back out to the gate and give the guy there your stub, okay? You come back in on ground level."

Avery was on her own now and she liked that. She smiled at me. An adult, she was kickin' now, livin' large. Life was a ride in a gerbil tube, or whatever else they called it on MTV.

"And no flirting with the ushers," Sammy called after her. "They've got a job to do."

I could only picture Avery's facial response to that.

"Your kid?" the receptionist asked.

"Some days," I told the truth.

"She's cute."

I'd have stayed around to discuss it, but Sammy was ushering me across the blue carpeting, into a vacant office with John Wathan's name on the door. We stood in front of the uncluttered executive desk. This was an office even Wathan never used. Sammy had closed the door.

"You got something to say to me?" he asked, no longer fiddling with the gold watch on his left wrist.

"Did you kill her?"

Sammy blinked, then focused his dark eyes on my lighter brown but steady stare. Sammy apparently saw nothing there to be afraid of. Looking harmless is a trick of mine.

"I could ask you the same question."

"You took her purse and jewelry," I said. "Did you clean the drinking glasses, too?"

"It's my job to take care of messes." He gave me a false smile. That's what lawyers do, all right. Trouble is they seem to enjoy it so much. The more trouble you're in, before you have to call one, the better.

"It's your job to diaper his butt?"

"Now you're catching on." This time Sammy's capped smile was for real. But it was gone in an instant. "I don't like you, Franklin. You're trouble for my boy. I don't know how you got over on him, but he wants you here today. Probably thinks you actually looked for his damn glove."

"Actually, I did."

"Then you should have found it."

"I guess so." I thought about the videotape. I wasn't ready to give that information away. If Sammy knew the tape existed, he'd as much as asked me about it. My jaw locked. My shoulders tensed. The red-faced agent paced away from me, then froze to consider my six-foot frame from a safe distance.

"I'd turn you in for this thing, Franklin. But it's over now."

There was assumed power in his voice, a leather whip and a wooden chair. This *thing* he talked about was Dorothy Fleming's murder. Threats from a scared teenager huddled in the back of a van were one thing. A threat face to face from a pompous manipulator was quite a different matter.

"You mess up my boy, you cause any trouble whatsoever, I'll do it," Sammy went on. "You got a record. You got a reputation in this city I've been hearing about ever since Marilyn told me you were coming to town. You fart in the wrong direction, I'm turning you over to the police. We'll take our chances with the newspapers."

"Or look at it like this, Sam. I'm the one turning you in."

"Don't even think about it, big boy. I had a reason to be there. I had a fucking appointment. You're a thief, pal. You were just robbing the place."

"You ever play the horses, Sam?" My eyes burned him, darkening the color of his paid-for tan.

He wasn't interested in answering.

"Let me tell you about the horses," I condescended. "You can plan a race right down to how many times the winning jockey is going to use the whip and in which hand. You can get it just right, a front-runner fading on a deep rail the day after a rain. Your horse coming out of the pack, gobbling him up. You can see it just like it's supposed to happen. And you know what?"

Sammy wouldn't play along. I told him anyway.

"It won't turn out that way. It won't turn out the way it's supposed to, the way you plan it."

But that wasn't the way it was in Sammy's world. He was in control. He called the shots. He wasn't buying my caveat. In fact, the little prick had a warning of his own.

"Do horses bite, Franklin?"

"Thoroughbreds do," I said. "And Shetland ponies."

"I do, Franklin. I bite. And when I bite, I don't let go."

Short guys learn to say that.

"What about Reno?" I asked, throwing in another figure to be handicapped.

"What about him?" Sammy nearly shouted.

"It'll make the papers, Sam."

"Fuck him, the cunt can't swim. It was an accident, Franklin. Rowdy didn't trust him anyway."

I filed that one on impact. Sammy Maxwell had finally

screwed up. He'd given out information. *Rowdy didn't trust him anyway.*

"Someone might talk," I said.

"Not you," Sammy shot right back. "Not Marilyn. Not Richard. And not Gary Wright. The girls upstairs are safe. And I don't think your girlfriend will do anything to hurt her sister. Do you? And your kid . . . hell, she doesn't even know what happened."

I didn't want to think otherwise about Avery, but someone should have told him not to underestimate thirteen-year-old girls. They have ears like elephants'.

"Who did I leave out?" Sammy asked smugly. "Oh yeah, Rowdy. Let me tell you about Rowdy. He cares about one thing, Franklin. One thing only. His fucking arm. You think he's got anything on his mind but what he wants to throw a clean-up hitter on the third pitch, I'm afraid you'd better stick to horses."

Short guys learn to jump. Sammy jumped down my throat with spikes on. He stepped closer, lowering his voice.

"Randall Monroe is the darling of the household, Franklin. Not you. Everyone at that house, hell, everyone in this city will say you did it before they'll even hint that Rowdy is even peripherally involved. And they'll say so in court. He's a hero, Franklin, a fucking hero. You don't believe me, you call the cops."

I believed him.

"You might not have to," Sammy said. "Things get any more complicated, I will call them myself. Put you in a paper sack like a turd and set you out on the curb. Tell the cops to come get you. You know what the cops do with turds? They have an unsanitary landfill in this state they call the hole."

There was a bubble of spit in the corner of Sammy's mouth. His cologne smelled like something that would kill flying insects at fifty paces.

"But you've already been in prison, haven't you. For all I know you're one of those perverted sociopaths who actually like it."

"I have the videotape," I finally said, having tired of the lawyer's performance.

Sammy's dark eyes flashed brief emotion.

"We'll be wanting that back." He pointed two mani-cured fingers of his left hand at my chest. I considered breaking both of them, then feeding him his fancy wrist-watch so he'd know in the future when it was time to shut up. "And the glove, while you're at it."

TWELVE

I finally met somebody who confessed giving a damn about Rowdy's baseball glove.

That was refreshing. It was no real surprise that Sammy Maxwell knew about the tape. I probably shouldn't have mentioned it, but I wanted Rowdy's den mother to know I had something on my side of the fence. I needed the edge. And the respect.

They'd found pornographic French prints in George Washington's desk the day after he died. Other than for their personal use, the police weren't concerned about homemade porn, unless it involved children. Adult porn was everywhere. T&A was the warp of the loom upon which the American fabric had been woven.

In this case, however, the video could be motive for murder. If not murder, blackmail, which in turn was motive for murder. As dumb as it sounded, I tried to keep in mind the fact that Rowdy Monroe had been in love with Dorothy Fleming.

More than anything, Rowdy had probably wanted to keep Marilyn from seeing the tape.

110

Besides pissing me off in a grand way, Sammy Maxwell had said too much. Reno Stouth being untrustworthy was one thing. Sammy having had an appointment with Dorothy Fleming was quite another. Perhaps the appointment had been to buy the tape back from Bird. It would have been one more instance of Rowdy's agent wiping the big leaguer's ass for him.

The shoes the clubhouse boy found for me were too small. They cramped my toes and I was forced to leave the laces untied. I walked pigeon-toed.

He dressed me as a batboy, so I could sit in the bull pen without the fans becoming curious. Other writers, I was told, had used this trick. As it turned out, Rowdy could ask for the favor no more than once a season. His earned-run average low enough, he was granted his wish.

The locker room smelled antiseptic, laced with expensive cologne. Damp towels and mildew thrived in the minor leagues, not at Royals Stadium. The room was nearly deserted. I marveled at the names and numbers on the partitioned dressing areas. What passed for lockers these days had room for furniture and, indeed, each was outfitted with a chair. I eyed the locker area labeled *Bo Jackson #16* as others might eye Lincoln's bedroom on a White House tour.

"Training room," the clubhouse attendant said. "The early birds are all in the training room. Strictly off-limits. They don't let Wathan in there, let alone reporters. They want to tell a dirty story, it's in there. They want to cry their eyes out, it's in the training room."

The clubhouse boy was about my age. He lit up a cigarette as soon as we were out of the locker room. We walked down a long corridor. I tried not to take baby steps in my too-tight shoes. There was an entire town under the seats at Royals Stadium. And it was painted blue.

"You want to write a book," the middle-aged attendant continued, "get a trainer to talk. Wait till he retires or something. Training room's where the real shit gets talked about."

I pictured Rowdy wrapped in a towel, taking a backrub on the training table, telling his teammates all about Dorothy Fleming, Reno Stouth, and his missing baseball glove. Ballplayers lived under an unstated vow of secrecy. I understood that. Being on a team was membership in a very exclusive club. Nobody outside the Show was worthy of confidence.

Wives were told less than reporters. Wives were on the outside. Sports reporters were let in the door with the clear understanding that they were inferior beings. Clubhouse pets. Wives weren't even let in the door. Their job was to look good in the seats set aside for them during play-off and championship games.

The clubhouse cadet and I approached a noise that had me quite curious. It sounded like someone throwing a wet sock against a concrete wall. There was a slow, delayed rhythm to the recurring sound.

Turning a corner on our way to the home dugout, I saw him. In an area off the walkway, a black man wearing gym shorts pulled back the pound-test string of a competition archery bow, an arrow in place, its feathers against his ear. I paused to watch.

Unlike Reno Stouth's bulging bulk, these were muscles that worked, that operated just right. Tendons, ligaments and flesh choreographed by someone better than

112

Balanchine. Standing still, Bo's was a body that danced. A body cocked.

His were muscles that ran faster, jumped higher and threw harder. Muscles in full command of bone and blood. Muscles that swung a piece of wood with the speed and power and accuracy to more than occasionally catch up with a ninety-five-mile-an-hour pitch. Someone told me once that hitting a major league fastball was like standing on the hood of a speeding car at night and eyeing an oncoming gnat illuminated momentarily in the headlights.

Not any ninety-five-mile-an-hour gnat would do. You had to hit that one. Swing!

In Bo's case, he accomplished the feat with both frightening power and absolute beauty. Mere motion. Even when he went down swinging, you wanted to watch him do it again. From a fan's point of view, Bo deserved two slots in the batting order.

There were four arrows in the target's bull's-eye. We watched Bo place a fifth in the inner circle. He was not an inaccurate type of man.

"Nice shot," my companion said, and with that we were on our way.

"He's done as many as twelve in a row," the boy told me. "He's after twenty, if there's room on the target. 'Bout now the arrows start hitting each other."

And people said Bo's hobby was football.

I attempted to lengthen my stride, to straighten out my knees with each step as I crimped by in my shoes. My body felt like a piece of toilet paper. Something you use once then throw away. My body was disposable, like Dorothy Fleming's. I should have a T-shirt made that read *Body by Reno*. The town, I mean. I'd lost my ass trying to bet the sports book there that features televised races from eight different tracks.

The fountains above and beyond the right-field fence hadn't been turned on yet. General Admit—the bleachers—had yet to open. The vendors hadn't shown up. And neither had the teams, though the cage was in place for batting practice.

I stood in the dugout and stared at the green turf rising above me like a swell of ocean. The pitcher's mound was more an island than a pedestal. The man out there once the game started would be stranded, trapped, entirely unto himself. Alone. John Donne hadn't known about major league baseball when he'd written his sermons.

"I wouldn't hang around on the field," the clubhouse attendant advised. "Someone might ask you to pick up the bats." And he was gone.

Standing in John Wathan's spot in the dugout, I picked up one of the telephones and punched nine. "Tell Quisenberry to warm up," I growled into the receiver, remembering another day, a previous season in Kansas City baseball.

It was the World Series and Herzog, the White Rat, was in the other dugout, along with a bunch of National League crybaby sissies they called a team. Hah! Me and Quiz would mow them down above the knees with that sidearm submarine. They called his pitches breaking balls because that's exactly what they did.

Marilyn answered the phone.

"This is Alton. I need to talk to Carolyn."

"I just got off the phone with Sammy. You seen the little bastard since?"

"No," I said, surprised by the venom in her voice. "It's probably better not to talk about that."

If her sister's voice was angry, Carolyn's was dark.

"We're going to the game, Alton. Can you believe it?"

"Yes."

"She's very upset. I don't think it's a good idea, but Marilyn says she *needs to*. I can't believe it."

"Reno?"

"What else? They were close friends, Alton. He helped her work out when he wasn't working with Rowdy. She wants to call his brother at the health club, but Sammy told her to wait. They're supposed to remove the body first."

"Maybe she already called him, Carolyn."

"What do you mean?"

"Listen, try to find out Reno's brother's name. Find out if it's Jim, okay?"

"Is that who you were talking about this morning? Is that the Jim you meant?"

"I think so."

"Well, it's not." Carolyn sounded certain. "I heard her refer to him as David. Yeah, it's David, now that I think about it. David Stouth."

"Damn." I switched tracks. "Carolyn, you think it's Reno she was having an affair with?"

"No." Carolyn sounded more certain. Confidant maybe. "He liked her. But nothing like that. You'd have seen it this morning at breakfast if they'd been, uh, you know, involved."

"You talk to him much?"

115

"Chitchat, that's all. He was a nice guy, Alton. A real sweetheart."

I thought of Sammy Maxwell's epitaph for the curly-haired bodybuilder. *Fuck him, the cunt can't swim.*

"Let me ask you something, then I have to run. They have me dressed up like a Little Leaguer and I'm looking for a place to hide."

"Okay."

"Does Marilyn know who Rowdy was fooling around with, specifically?"

"Let me think . . . yeah, she seemed to. She talked as if there were only one woman and she seemed to have a particular person in mind. He'd been messing around on the road. I guess they all do. When Marilyn became pregnant, he told her it was all over, that he'd ended it. Hey, what are you getting at? You think Marilyn killed her?"

"No. She was at the game too."

"Right, buddy. And don't you forget it."

"One more thing. You know Gary's last name? Richard's friend?"

"The fat kid? No, I don't."

"I didn't think so."

"Is that it?" Carolyn sounded confused.

"Drive the van out, will you? The spare key's under the rear bumper, left side, magnetic—"

"I know," Carolyn cut in. "You showed me a hundred times."

"You want to, you can throw our bags in. We could leave from the game."

"I think we'd better stay. I don't think we should leave Marilyn alone right yet. She's going through with the reading tonight."

"The what?"

"The reading. Didn't someone tell you? The reading at the house tonight."

"Séance?"

"Alton! *Poetry* reading. Once a month the people in Marilyn's writing class meet at someone's house. It's important to her, Alton. She's going to read for the first time. Her own stuff."

"I'm looking forward to it," I lied. A poetry reading made drinking lighter fluid and swallowing lit matches sound good.

"You will be there. Nobody ducks out. Even Rowdy's going to make it."

"Well, listen, don't load up the van with people, okay? I don't want to end up car-pooling everyone home. On second thought, you'd better drive out alone. Something embarrassing might slide out from under the seats."

"Hey, dickface!" someone shouted from the dugout corridor. "What the hell you doing on the phone? Get away from that!"

It was one of the players.

"Got to go," I said, and hung up. I kept my back to the Royals second-stringer as best I could, feeling pale and old and out of shape. The player slid on by and waltzed out onto the field as if the sunshine had been waiting for him to make an appearance.

I pulled my ballcap down to my ears, climbed out of the dugout and quickly checked to see if Avery had yet to find her seat. She hadn't. I slouched pigeon-toed toward the right-field bull pen. It was a long walk. I kept close to the stadium wall that separated the seats from the playing field, praying the bull-pen gate was unlocked.

THIRTEEN

The Brewers took batting practice, working on the longball to right field. I couldn't read the numbers but it might have been Rob Deer, the home-run power of the Milwaukee team, who banged away in the cage. Or Paul Molitor. Now that he'd been relegated to designated hitter, Molitor probably worked on the longball as well. Whoever, the balls were coming right at me.

The fountains had come on for a pre-game test and a fine spray of cool moisture drifted into the Royals bull pen. The crowd, too, was showing up. There was a lot of noise coming from the right-field General Admit seats high above the bull pen. The organist practiced his numbers. It felt like baseball, like something big was about to happen.

"Who's that?" I asked the guy slouched next to me in the bull-pen seats as a hit ball rolled against the chain-link between us and the field of play.

"Charlie O'Brien," Billy Lee Burke drawled. "They all hit the longball in batting practice. Working out the kinks. Once they face real pitchin', Frank White will scoop up the crap that comes off their bats, they keep trying for right field."

Billy Lee was the old-timer on the pitching staff. He had begun the young season in the starting rotation but had trouble going more than three innings. As soon as somebody got hot in Omaha, the Royals were likely to call up the kid and send Burke down.

"They're startin' to call left field here the Bermuda Triangle. They hit one short of a homer, the ball disappears. But I tell you what, they're startin' to hope Bo catches the damn thing right off. It falls in front of or behind him and Bo throws them out at second or third."

"Or home," I said, remembering a Bo Jackson throw from deep left to Bob Boone's glove to tag a Seattle player coming for a sure score in the ninth inning. It would have been the tying run.

"Don't matter," Burke said, spitting tobacco juice between his own feet. "Bo'll end up in center field. He's still, what you call, in training."

"There any way out of here during a game?"

"You either get called to the mound or you sit out the whole show right here. Only way in and only way out of the bull pen is across the playing field."

A hard-hit ball bounced low into the chain-link and I instinctively ducked, drawing my feet back from the tall fence. Burke didn't bat an eye.

"Unless of course you can scale the wall into General Admit," he added. "Some have tried."

"But you could walk out during a game? I mean, if you had to."

Burke shook his head. "They'd fine you. The crowd would get on your ass, too."

"No one's ever done it?"

Burke spit again. "I didn't say that. There was one fella once who put on a batboy outfit like yours and left at the seventh-inning stretch while the crew were rakin' the infield. Did it another time during a rain delay."

"Who's that?"

Burke gave me a hard look. "You'll have to get that story from somebody else. I didn't say a word about it."

I figured Billy Lee Burke was telling on himself. He wanted to boast but he didn't want a writer to use the story. The balls kept coming our way.

"You know Sammy Maxwell?" I tried.

"Is that what you're up to? You workin' on that stuff about agents signing kids while they're still in high school."

"No. I'm doing a magazine piece on Rowdy. Maxwell's his agent."

"Maxwell's what's left in the jar when you circumcise a prick," Burke said, eyes on the field. "All those lawyers are. You want to write I said that"—he spat more brown juice between his shoes—"you go right ahead."

"You stay at the Regal?"

"Everyone does," Burke said. "Those agents got pus for blood, you know that? They're an infection walking around lookin' for a place to happen. It's like paying somebody to cut your dick off for you with a rusty can-op'ner."

Gee, I wasn't the only one who didn't like Sammy Maxwell.

"You know Dorothy Fleming?"

"Everyone did. Sad story, ain't it? Let me say this, you want to bleed to death in a big hurry you sign up with one of those agents. Full of maggots. You slice open that Maxwell fella and what you get is a mess of maggots where the rest of us have hearts."

"Rowdy's got it, wouldn't you say?" I asked, trying to play the writer.

"He's cookin'."

"The heat, I mean. He really throws smoke."

Burke spat more juice. "Let me fill you in on that. It takes meat *and* heat to be cookin'. You have to place that ball in the meat of the plate."

"Anybody can throw a fastball?"

"Shit no. Almost nobody can. But the ones that do, they have to learn to place the ball, to move it around and use the corners, or the big bats will knock them out of the park. Thing about an ninety-mile-an-hour pitch is it gets over the center-field fence in a big rush."

"Rowdy has both, then. Heat and meat?"

"That he does."

"Just like you," I tossed in diplomatically.

"I throw shit pitches," Burke corrected me. "I'm what you call a contact pitcher. It's all deception, mixed deliveries, backward spin on the balls. I throw 'em shit and they make contact. A good infield, a catcher quick to chase pop-ups behind the plate, I get my outs."

"You make it sound like a circus act."

Burke laughed. "That's exactly what it is. I tell you, you set up a pitching machine that throws hundred-and-ten-mile-per-hour strikes to alternating corners of the strike zone. After three pitches, half the guys on this team'll be knocking 'em out of the park every pitch. They know what's coming, they time the release, they can homer fastballs wearing a gorilla suit."

Were I a writer, I'd have been taking this down.

"It ain't the arm, you want to know the truth. Pitchin' in the big leagues ain't the arm. It's the legs. You ever see how a pitcher comes down on his leg?"

I nodded.

"Most people throwin' a ball that hard would fall on their face. Your leg tires out, the speed starts comin' off the throw. It don't matter how good your arm is. Guy breaks his wrist, he can still pitch if his legs are up to it. A little adjustment in the throw is all. You move it off the palm."

I wondered about Billy Lee Burke's legs.

"Arm, legs, shit man, it's the whole body. It's like your entire body is born with the coordination to throw that ball or it ain't. When it goes haywire, your whole body jams up. I seen a guy, he knocked his shoulder out comin' down wrong at the end of a pitch. And it wasn't even his throwin' arm."

I waited for him to wind down. How did you get these guys to shut up?

"He didn't fall down or nothin'. Just came down hard. A little off and his shoulder popped out. Screamed like a dog had took a chew of his testicles."

Burke paused to spit.

"You know Rowdy's little brother?" I asked. "Has he got it?"

The older pitcher almost laughed. "He's just tall, that's all. No chance in hell he'll make the Show."

"All pitchers are tall now," I said. "Isn't that what it takes?"

"Shit no. They just recruit that way around here. Royals want the whole athlete. Like you buy horses by how tall they are, but it ain't got a whole lot to do with who wins the race."

You had to like a person who came up with horse analogies.

"They got midgets down in the Dominican Republic can strike out Brett. But they make lousy baseball cards, you know what I'm sayin'?"

The baseballs had stopped coming. The Royals were up to take batting practice. Local news reporters in brightly colored blazers were trailed by cameramen toward the cage. Traffic stacked up on the highway. Sunday afternoon games in good weather sold out in Kansas City as often as they didn't in bad weather.

Burke stood up to spit, retrieving his glove. "Got to go lollygag." He looked at me straight-on for a moment and, without smiling, said, "Pull up that cap a tad. You look like Gomer Pyle."

I felt like Gomer Pyle. I wondered if a person's entire body was born with the coordination to murder. Heat and meat. A gun and a little bit of guts was all it took. Maybe murder was something you learned only if you had to.

Sammy was at the scene of the murder. So was Bird. The kid might have shot her out of desperation, but desperation makes people awkward. There was nothing awkward about Dorothy Fleming's death.

That left Jim and . . . Anyone could have hired him.

Marilyn had made a call to the man and so had Bird. As the parking lots filled to capacity, I was captivated by the apparent connection between Carolyn's poetry-loving sister and a fourteen-year-old car thief.

"Shazam!" I said out loud. Bird's theft of the

Monroemobile was a setup. That's why he'd stolen it from the driveway in the middle of the morning. Bird had been paid to steal it. By a man named Jim? Whoever wanted the car stolen had wanted the videotape. Bird caught on and that's when everything went bonkers.

I attempted to adjust my cap to look more like a professional. The day smelled like baseball. The crowd was noisy. Bats cracked from the cage on the field. What a sport. Baseball, where the possibility of what could miraculously be, could magnificently have been, exists at the bare edges of what is, another scoreless inning, another boring pop-up. A sentence wanting verb.

Anyone could have hired Jim. And anyone could have pushed Reno Stouth into a swimming pool with two deep ends.

The police didn't talk to Carolyn. The ambulance had come and gone.

Stan Gardner, a tall attorney from Maxwell's firm, showed up to control what Marilyn, Richard and Gary said to the police. It wouldn't look like an accidental death if the lawyer refused to let them answer a few questions. Reports would be typed, signed.

Following the officers' departure in a tasteful, unmarked sedan, Gardner gathered the group in Marilyn's sitting room.

"There are two ways to drown," he said. "One is to fill your lungs with water."

Carolyn didn't care for his casual use of the word *your.* He could keep the damn water out of her lungs, thank you.

"The other," he continued, "is to smother. That's

when the water outside your body keeps you from being able to breathe. It happens this way most often when a person is unconscious, face-down in water."

Everyone in the room seemed anxious to leave. Sandra and Julie sported bright summer outfits, sorority-roof tans, cautious smiles. Richard was brave and stoic. Marilyn had withdrawn within herself. She chain-smoked. And Gary fidgeted with his hands, avoiding eye contact with anyone.

Alton had asked if Carolyn knew Gary's last name. It was doubtful she'd ever heard it. She remembered that even Sammy had had trouble coming up with the poor slob's first name when they'd been given their instructions in the rumpus room.

"We'll wait to see what the coroner says. Either way, it's very clear this was an accidental death. It was well known that Mr. Stouth couldn't swim. And that nasty lick he took in the fall . . ." Gardner trailed off, nodding to himself.

He cleared his throat to add, "It's likely there will be no further investigation by the police. None is required. However, there may be an insurance investigation, depending on whether Mr. Stouth had a sizable policy."

No one was listening. Gardner raised his voice in pitch.

"In this event, I advise each of you not to talk with the investigator. And, should a news reporter become interested, don't say a word. Call our office and give us the reporter's name. We'll take care of it from there."

Damage control, Carolyn thought. Death was one hell of an inconvenience for people in the public eye. From the look of Gardner's jewelry and hand-tooled shoes, it was going to be an expensive inconvenience for Rowdy and Marilyn as well.

"One more thing." Gardner held up a lone finger, making sure they got the number right. "Nobody goes to the funeral. Family members at this time may act in unexpected ways."

Marilyn shot him a nasty glare through the blue smoke of her burning cigarette.

"They may blame you for his death because he died here," Gardner explained. "We have to avoid a scene. Of course, flowers will be sent. We'll be certain your condolences are paid."

Marilyn had a condolence of her own. Carolyn watched her younger sister lift her lone finger in response to the attorney's summation. He nodded politely and left the room.

Outdoors it was a beautiful day. In defeat of death, Carolyn wore a beautiful dress. It was a new sundress of crisp cotton she'd spent the morning ironing. Belted, open-necked, with a mid-calf skirt, the clean white material was printed with vertical stripes of pastel blue and pink. It showed off her skin, her dark hair, her blue eyes, and she looked pretty wearing it.

Richard and Gary and their girlfriends took Gary's Jeep, the one in which they'd come to town, to the ballpark. Marilyn was taking the Volvo. Carolyn had the engine started when she realized someone else was inside Alton's van. Again. Only he wasn't hiding this time.

Marilyn backed the Volvo out of the driveway. Carolyn couldn't let her get away. She was a moment from laying on the horn when the kid in the back said, "Wait! I need your help. I need it bad."

Carolyn caught a glimpse of him in the rearview mirror. He was crouched in the middle of the back of the van. She turned off the key, prepared to hop out and walk away. He'd have to shoot her in the back in broad daylight.

"Please," he pleaded, starting to rise. "They're going to kill me. You have to help me."

FOURTEEN

The stadium was packed. And the bull pen was crowded. I sheepishly occupied a seat at the far end, just under the fountains and away from General Admit. Fans hung over the wall, shouting encouragement, attempting to trick the relievers into looking up. Billy Lee Burke sat next to me but wasn't saying a word now that the game had started. Gubicza had the mound.

Rowdy had less to say than Burke, choosing to ignore me altogether. But then, he wasn't really talking to any-one. He appeared calm, almost serene. I could imagine the butterflies that ate at the left-hander's intestines. If butterflies had teeth, they were the ones.

So far, I'd learned that effective pitching in the Show had as much to do with deception as with any particular skill. Oh yeah, and legs. Pitchers were the Rockettes of major league baseball.

One of the overhanging fans called for "Blind Boy" time and time again. Rowdy apparently never heard him. He might have had earplugs attached to his glasses.

The crowd practiced the Wave for no apparent reason.

It was a Sunday crowd of tourists. The weekend draw to Royals games was more than half from out of town. Nebraska, Iowa and western Kansas license plates populated the parking lots.

I thought I could see Avery's feather of blue hair behind the home-team dugout, but it might have been a mirage. I also thought I could rather easily play right field if I had to. Nothing much happened out here. I should have brought along Rowdy's glove. Of course, I'd have to play left-handed, but I could handle that. All you did in right field was stand around and look interested. It was a daydreamer's place to be.

"Where's your gun?"

"I hid it in back," Bird said, climbing into the passenger's seat. "I didn't mean to scare you. They're after me. I need to talk to Rooster, but I need a favor first."

"I'm not going anywhere until you apologize," Carolyn said.

"You don't understand. This ain't no game. They tore up my apartment. They're waiting for me."

"Like I said . . ."

"Hey, I didn't kill the woman if that's what you're thinking. That's all a big mistake. I didn't kill nobody. Me and Rooster, we're working on this one together. That's why he wasn't going to turn me in, you see? I'm on your side."

"You're supposed to apologize," she reminded him. "Does your mother know where you are right now?"

"Aw shit," Bird groaned. "You're one of those. I'm sorry, all right? Look, let me drive. It'll be quicker."

"You're not old enough to drive."

"What? Did Rooster tell you everything?" Bird slapped his forehead. "Lady, I'm running for my life here, okay? And you want to see my birth certificate or something!"

"I'm Carolyn Sakwoski. I'm sorry but I've forgotten your name."

"Bird, right? Look—"

"Your name?"

"You can't turn me in! Look, Carolyn, it's not safe in that house. You need to know that. There's a bunch of bad shit going around and I'm in the middle of it. So, okay, you drive, all right? But let's get going."

"I'm waiting."

"Robin," Bird relented. "It's a guy's name. Robin Bunter." Bird quickly shifted his gaze, scanning the street out the passenger window.

The boy had the Batman logo shaved into the back of his head. Just wait till Avery meets this one, Carolyn thought.

"What's the big favor, Robin?"

"Oh man, call me Bird, okay? I'm trying to save my life here and you act like I'm up for adoption."

"Don't get smart. You want the favor, not me."

"I'm sorry again, all right? I need a ride, that's all. I thought you might be cool, you know."

Carolyn smiled to herself. She hadn't heard anyone say *cool* in a long while. She put the van in gear.

"One thing you should know. Alton rigged this van with a bomb. All I have to do is push a switch, get out and walk away. Fifteen seconds and the whole thing goes up. Once that switch is pushed, it's set. You can't turn it off."

"Who's Alton?"

"Rooster," Carolyn said, disappointed that Bird hadn't been impressed by her fable.

"Right. Let's go already. We ain't got all day."

Carolyn turned to face him and their eyes locked. He's just a kid, she thought. He isn't shaving yet.

"If you ever point a gun at me again, I'll slap you until you fall down."

"Anyone ever tell you, you got nice hair?"

It was difficult to concentrate on the game. They needed a television out here for you to see what was going on. The other bull-pen occupants weren't all that interested in the Royals' at-bats. When the Brewers were at the plate, however, they became engrossed in the distant players, the number of pitches, the swings.

Gubicza looked to me to be throwing bullets. The Brewers had yet to fire a shot in return.

My thoughts drifted. I chose up sides, dividing the Monroe marriage into two teams. There was Rowdy on one bench, Marilyn on the other. Both were having affairs, Rowdy with a dead woman, Marilyn with a man unknown. Her lover was not, according to Carolyn, Reno Stouth.

The roster of Rowdy's team was pretty clear. Marilyn disliked Sammy Maxwell, making the agent a favorite for team captain. Then came the blood and the hangers-on. Richard Monroe, Gary Wright, Sandra and Julie. Throw in all the ballplayers and the Royals front office, the thousands of local fans, and Rowdy fielded a formidable team indeed.

On Marilyn's side, there was Carolyn.

To my own regret, I hadn't found Marilyn easy to like.

And she apparently liked me even less. Whatever role I played in this game, it wasn't as a member of either team.

Also playing for Marilyn was her unknown boyfriend. Or maybe Carolyn had been wrong about Marilyn having an affair. I doubted it. Sisters weren't usually wrong about such things. Of course, Marilyn was carrying the Rookie of the Year in her womb. Rowdy didn't have a player who possessed the power of an offspring.

Reno Stouth remained an enigma. He'd been Rowdy's personal trainer. Hang around Rowdy long enough, all of ten minutes, and he told you everything. Reno and Marilyn had somehow become friends. Carolyn had suggested they might be confidants. No wonder Sammy Maxwell didn't trust the bodybuilder.

Of course Marilyn Monroe knew about Dorothy Fleming's bedding her husband on the road. And if Rowdy believed he'd loved the woman, she probably knew that too. Reno had been the go-between.

That left Bird and a stranger named Jim out of the batting order. Bird was hired to steal Rowdy's car. Whose side did that place him on? No one's, I decided. The teenage terror had already admitted to negotiating with Dorothy Fleming on his own. He'd been hired to steal the car and hand over what was in the trunk and he hadn't. Someone had to be upset about that.

The Royals were at bat in the bottom of the second when I was caught once again daydreaming on first. I smelled something burning before I felt it. By then, it was too late to do anything but dance.

The kid was too young to be dangerous. He wore a bright yellow T-shirt under the red leather jacket. It was a warm day, but Carolyn suspected it was never too warm to look cool. His dark eyes, always darting, seemed to know what he was going to see before he saw it. The kid was cute, but tense.

Alton had told her Bird was personally responsible for the doubling of automobile-comprehensive insurance premiums in three zip codes. She doubted it. Carolyn was also certain, having spent more time around Bird without a gun in his hand, that he hadn't shot Dorothy Fleming. Bird was too young to have shot anyone.

He continued giving her directions and Carolyn played along.

"What were the cops doing at the house?"

Bird looked anywhere but at Carolyn. He asked questions he was vitally interested in, but worked hard to make it appear as nothing more than idle chatter. Alton doesn't understand children, she thought. They make a crisis of the smallest thing. Every problem is the stuff of high drama.

"A friend of the family's drowned."

"Who?" Bird asked quickly.

"Reno Stouth. He was Rowdy's personal trainer."

"Damn, damn, damn," Bird muttered. He drummed his fingers on the dashboard.

"Did you know him?"

"*Body by Reno*, everybody knows him. What you mean he drowned? Is he . . . dead?"

Body of Reno, Carolyn thought grimly. Alton was right, of course. They should leave town after the game. But she couldn't abandon Marilyn. In a day or two, if her sister were holding up . . .

"Yes," Carolyn answered his question plainly. "It was

an accident. He slipped and fell into the pool, banged his head."

"Accident, my ass. Turn here, left!"

Carolyn drove Bird into midtown. He'd directed her south of the sports complex, avoiding traffic. They picked up Linwood Boulevard, driving west toward Broadway and Main. The old city, the east side, rose up around them in burned-out buildings and vacant lots, punctuated by the occasional block of struggling residential sections. Many yards were weedy, some of the houses boarded up. Many were not.

On a corner where they stopped for a light, two middle-aged men in white T-shirts handed a quart of beer between each other and leered openly at Carolyn. One of them said something she couldn't make out. Carolyn pushed the control that locked all the doors of the van, startling Bird.

"I didn't want to bring this up," Bird said, looking at her this time, then rapidly away. "But are you and Rooster married or what?"

I was cooking. Literally.

My pants were on fire. Heat and meat, only I was the meat. I leapt to my feet, nearly falling over in my borrowed shoes, and swatted at my rear end with my cap. One of the relievers had hotfooted my back pocket. I whooped it up, looking for a bucket of Gatorade to sit down in.

It burned like crazy. No one offered to help. Rowdy leaned against the bull-pen wall and blinked through his thick lenses at my death-defying tap dance. He was going in today. He could do without the stunt.

The burned cloth smoldered. And it kept burning. One of the bull-pen regulars opened the gate. Another hollered, "Water in the dugout!"

I shot out into the arena like a rodeo bull, high-stepping. I fanned. I tripped. I fell on the turf. It felt nothing like grass. I rolled over like a log, and over again, making sure I'd put myself out.

A sinner on his way to hell catching a glimpse of paradise, I could see the fountains above and beyond the outfield fence. I'd need wings or Jacob's ladder to make it to those pools of cool water.

The home-plate umpire threw both arms toward sky in mid-pitch and stepped away from behind the plate. I was hit by half-full beer cups from General Admit. The ump's arms stayed there, as if he were holding an invisible sign above his head. Time-out for the occasional distraction tossed onto the field of play. A drunken batboy. I made it to my feet, the TV cameras picking me up.

The Brewer playing right field wisely backed away. Uniformed security guards jogged toward me in tandem. A cup of beer hit me in the head and the General Admit seats cheered. The organ played something dumb.

Head bowed, cap off, I slouched toward bedlam, toward the jeering fans. I was showered with beers as soon as I came near enough. The stands applauded hysterically amid dog-woofs and catcalls.

Soon, but not soon enough, they had me by the arms. My hair beer-soaked, I was escorted off the field by the baseball cops. It was a black day for batboys everywhere.

Still, there was plenty of joy in Mudville. I'd never heard front-on forty thousand six hundred and twenty-three people laugh simultaneously. It was a riot. It sounded like jumbo jets landing and taking off. I held out hope that Avery wouldn't recognize her beer-soaked dad.

At least I hadn't fallen into a backyard swimming pool and drowned, I thought. And neither, I finally decided, had Reno Stouth.

FIFTEEN

I was held in the security office for what seemed like several hours. You could feel the rise and fall of the crowd's ovations through the floor and walls. Sammy Maxwell eventually intervened. The security officer seemed disappointed she wouldn't be allowed to press charges against the middle-aged batboy who'd used his position of privilege to ruin America's good time at the ballpark. The same clubhouse boy who'd escorted me to the dugout came round to escort me back to the locker room.

"Are they ever pissed off at you," he said. "Might be the last time anyone but staff gets into the bull pen for a game."

I didn't have a thing to say to him. I pried off the killer shoes and quickly undressed.

"You might have to pay for these," the loyal employee said when I handed him the singed pair of pants.

"Put it on Maxwell's account."

"Is that a tattoo?" the attendant asked, eyeballing my chest.

"Birthmark."

I stepped into the shower stall to wash away the beer and at least part of the residual humiliation. The warm water stung the tender red blotch that now decorated one buttock. Some people ate beef cooked less than my backside. If someone had launched a live grenade into the home-team bull pen that afternoon, I wouldn't have been upset to hear about it.

"Keep going, keep going," Bird urged. They rolled by his apartment building on Linwood. "Okay now, pull up between those two buildings."

Carolyn did as he suggested. The driveway opened onto a small, paved turnaround where the trash dumpsters were kept. She circled the van and pulled back up the drive. As the nose of the van edged just past the buildings, Bird told her to stop.

"They won't recognize the van," he said. "Did you see the building? The white one. Second floor on the right, number 202." He gave her his key.

"It's a long walk from here," Carolyn protested. "If they're watching your place—"

"They'll think you live there," Bird cut her off. "Walk in like you're in a hurry. Maybe you have to pee or something. Lots of girls live in the building. Put some strut in it and they'll think you belong."

"Did you see them?" Carolyn asked, having second thoughts about Bird's plan.

"Yeah, he's in the black Ford, half a block up on the other side of the building. You know what to do?"

"Get a table knife out of the top drawer in the

kitchen," she recited. "Pull back the quarter-round in the bedroom closet."

"Far left corner. It's a loose piece, only one finishing nail's holding it."

"Roll back the carpet."

"Between the carpet and pad," Bird reminded her. "A brown envelope. Stick it in your underwear or something, you know, like that girl in Washington who worked for, uh, what's his name?"

"Oliver North."

"Right, then get back here and we're gone."

"Just one thing, Bird. If they get close to me, I'll give them the envelope. I'm not going to risk getting hurt."

"No sweat, sister," he said, faking it. "Just swing your rear a little when you walk, okay? You know, like you're selling it."

"No sweat, bro," Carolyn said right back. "Babes are born with it." She winked at him in a large way and climbed out of the van.

Bird piled into the driver's seat. Carolyn swung it down the sidewalk, adrenaline pumping. She watched the black car. She disliked having to walk toward it. A car driving by honked at her. She didn't know whether to smile or frown. If only she had a piece of gum to chew, she might manage the charade. Might even get an offer on the way into Bird's building.

There was a thrill to doing something clandestine in the middle of a sunny day. Hell, she thought, she should take up thievery and let Alton run the bookstore.

The man in the black Ford didn't turn to watch her. Knowing she wasn't being watched took some of the fun out of it. There didn't seem to be any danger.

Bird said he'd gone next door to celebrate a score yesterday. With a tenant of the building. After she'd left for work, which he'd carefully explained wasn't in the morning, he was still in her apartment when he heard them burst into his. Bird slipped out the back of the building through a door that only opened from the inside and was afraid to return—he'd have to use the front door.

He'd spent the night in a motel. The black Ford was out there when he came back by this morning.

Bird also told her that what was in the envelope would help Alton. Bird believed they were trying to set up his partner for Dorothy's murder. Partner? Carolyn considered the various things Alton would say in response to that suggestion, none of them polite. Bird wouldn't tell her what was in the envelope. He only repeated, "I can clear your boyfriend."

When she pushed the key into his lock, the door to Bird's apartment swung open on its own. It was dark inside. He'd warned her not to turn on the lights. Carolyn stepped in.

The place had been trashed. Furniture was broken into pieces. Stereo components lay smashed in the middle of the room. The big-screen television had been toppled. Stepping over a piece of chair, Carolyn caught a whiff of Old Spice cologne. By the time she heard the movement behind her, a man's muscled arm was already around her neck. She couldn't scream. She couldn't do anything.

"I'm not going to hurt you," the husky voice said. His breath stank. Carolyn didn't believe him. Her head spun. "All I want is the kid."

Carolyn Sakwoski, bookseller, milked the last drops of her courage in an effort to breathe. Her eyes became a camera, picking up sharply focused details of little importance. His arm holding her against him, he ruined the crisp cotton of Carolyn's dress front, wadded it, stained the material with the dreadful, overpowering odor of fear.

Richard Monroe and Gary Wright sat to either side of their girlfriends from Wichita State, three rows behind the home-team dugout. In front of them, sitting primly upright, Marilyn posed sentry over three empty seats that opened onto the aisle.

I slid in beside her. Richard and one of the girls said hello. Gary appeared to be glowering, but I was beginning to realize that he always did. Sandra and Julie, I wasn't certain which was which, wore halters that didn't. Marilyn looked at me and I nearly forgot what I was there for.

I needed the van. I was going to give Sammy the videotape and be done with it. I might even throw in the glove. Maybe he wanted to have it framed.

"Where's Avery?"

"She's around, Alton. I think she went up to the press box. Sammy got her in. Should be right back. Such a lovely girl."

Marilyn's eyes were the same color of blue as Carolyn's, but there was a different beauty in Marilyn's lidded gaze. Maybe she didn't, but her eyes knew what you were thinking. She was making me ask.

"Where's Carolyn?"

"Oh, she hasn't arrived yet. Perhaps she needed some time to herself."

"She hasn't arrived?"

141

"I gave her her ticket. She can come when she wants. Oh dear, you're worried. It's nothing serious, I'm sure. She was going to follow me out here and changed her mind. Carolyn's a big girl, Alton."

"Bring Avery home with you, will you? I need to go."

"Aren't you going to watch Rowdy pitch? He's sure he'll be given the close today."

Missing the Rowdy Monroe Show without flood or famine for cause was clearly family sacrilege punishable by pouts. Marilyn had a cute one. I started to say something about needing to talk with her, but this was neither the time nor the place.

There were long lines at the concession stands. I pushed my way along the inside of a circular descending ramp. The shortest distance between two points was a series of tight turns at Royals Stadium. Surveying the paved acreage of thousands upon thousands of private vehicles gleaming in the afternoon sunshine, I wanted very badly to steal one. As badly as I wanted a cigarette.

I knew where I was going now. I was going to move my daydreaming butt off first base. And I only needed a car to get there.

She and Bird were folded into the trunk of a car.

There'd been two men. If they had weapons, Carolyn hadn't seen one as they pushed her out of the building. Bird had pulled the van up in front. He didn't move when they came outside with Carolyn. He didn't do anything.

"I didn't want 'em to hurt you," he said. Bird's breath was warm on the back of Carolyn's neck. The car was moving.

"I thought you had a gun." Carolyn was angry for a moment as alternate emotions struggled against an over-riding fear. She wanted to be better than this in a crisis.

"I couldn't get it in time. You go waving guns around and somebody will kill you. They would have taken it out on you."

"Don't say that word." Carolyn shuddered. Her knees were cramped. At least they hadn't tied her hands. When they opened the trunk of the Ford, she'd leap at them with her fingernails. She'd tear their eyes out.

"They're not going to kill us," Bird insisted, trying to soothe her in the close darkness.

"I told you not to use that word!"

They hit a bump. Carolyn's body bit into the metal-work under the carpet. She'd always wondered why trunks were carpeted. Now she knew it was for the com-fort of kidnap victims.

"Shh," Bird said, squeezing against her. "You get too loud, they'll hear us."

"Don't you know how to fight?" Carolyn asked, angry again.

"Not these guys." His arm was around her loosely. The kid was trying to be brave, trying to protect her.

"Who are they? What do they want?"

"The big guy's David Stouth. He wants to know who killed his brother. He might also want a videotape he thought I had."

"You used that word again!"

"Shhh. Keep it down, will you?"

The car turned a corner. The worst part was when they came to a stop and the air turned instantly still in-

143

side the trunk. Her body was coated in a sheen of sweat. But that might have been fear.

Soon they were moving again and Carolyn could breathe.

"But what do they want with us?"

"I don't know. A trade or something."

"What about the envelope?"

"Forget it. It's something I need. It's not what they want."

"I don't believe you."

"You don't have to," Bird said quickly, "but it won't do either one of us any good to mention it in front of them."

"I wouldn't dream of it," Carolyn said. Unless she thought they'd let her go. Which she didn't. David Stouth and his helpers hadn't bothered to hide their faces. They were either confident sons of bitches or they were going to kill her and Bird before it was over.

Surely people in the apartments on Linwood looked out their windows from time to time. Surely someone in the other cars driving by had seen them being forced into the trunk. Surely someone had called 911 with the license-plate number.

This is all Alton's fault, she decided. He found some strange and criminal way to ruin her short vacation at her sister's house. Maybe Marilyn was right and Carolyn should find people other than ex-cons and gamblers as friends. Either way, Carolyn certainly wouldn't be traveling with Alton again. If she had a future to be traveling in.

"You feel kind of good," Bird said softly, pressing up against Carolyn.

"Cool it, Bird," she said blankly. "I'm old enough to be

your parole officer. And put your hand back on the end of your arm or I'll break your wrist."

"But if we're going to die . . ."

"You don't want to die a virgin, is that it? Well, tough luck, kid. You didn't, by any chance, leave a note in the van? Something to help out?"

"I didn't think of it," Bird confessed, his arm once again around Carolyn, exploring the darkness. Carolyn would never forgive Alton for this. Even if he showed up at the very next corner to let her out. Then it occurred to Carolyn that they might never be let out. They'd sell the car to Salvadoran refugees with her and Bird, or what was left of their bodies, still locked in the trunk.

"Bird, if you don't stop that this instant, I'm going to find your balls and pinch them off!"

"Promises, promises," he chided under his breath.

Carolyn had had enough. She struggled sideways under his arm. It didn't help any that they were crammed together hip-to-hip. That she'd chosen this day of all days to wear a dress. And it didn't seem to make any difference to her would-be seducer that she smelled of sweat.

His hand was on her thigh now, not pressing, only touching, lying there. Where was her dress anyway? It felt as if it were wrapped around her throat. If he reached her panty line, Carolyn vowed, she'd do something he would regret. Bird would end up with certain items of the male anatomy he could bowl with.

"Listen, Bird, it's bad enough being kidnapped. This isn't a bomb shelter. And I don't have sex in trunks. I don't have sex with strangers. And I would never have sex with an indecent person." She decided to leave his age out of it. Children didn't like being reminded.

145

Bird's hand froze. A bomb shelter? It sounded like something in an old movie. The car stopped at another intersection. Exhaust fumes filled their allotment of breathable air.

"What do you mean, indecent?" he asked.

"If you were any sort of a decent human being, you'd take off your jacket and let me use it as a pillow."

The car bounced. Carolyn had had it with this kid. Bird certainly possessed the will to live. So did she, dammit! First chance she had, she'd rip the big man's eyes out. She'd order a chainsaw from Sears. Then she'd find Alton and let him know in precise terms exactly what he'd put her through.

SIXTEEN

As far as Carolyn's sister was concerned, I tried not to hold a grudge. I'd had every good intention of liking Marilyn Monroe. It just hadn't worked out that way. You don't have to like a woman to enjoy looking at her. I saw the van parked on Linwood before the cab pulled up in front of Bird's apartment building.

"This is fine. Let me out." The cab stopped without pulling over to the curb. I passed forward a damp, wadded twenty from my front pocket, climbed out and jogged to the van. It was unlocked. The key was in the ignition. Carolyn knew better.

Bird had needed something when he showed up in the van this morning at the Monroe house. I should have guessed that what he'd needed was help. The kid must have called the house and talked her into coming over. I checked my hiding places and found both the glove and videotape, along with my other secret toys, intact. I also found a chrome automatic wedged in a corner of the fold-out bench-bed.

There was reason to hurry. I locked the van, pocketing

the spare key, and approached Bird's building in a trot. I hid Bird's gun inside my shirt and had to hold it in place to keep it from falling out as I fought hard not to flat-out run. I was going to hang that kid out the window by his heels.

The car stopped. One man got out and opened what sounded like an overhead garage door. The car pulled forward, over a bump. Carolyn listened intently. The Ford bottomed out with a sharp bang that echoed inside the trunk. She imagined they were driving into a freight car.

Her stomach tightened. The other man got out of the car and slammed his door shut, rocking the Ford. Carolyn was holding her breath. She could feel her pulse in her fingertips. She could feel Bird's body tense next to her. She wanted to say something about fighting for their freedom once they were let out of the trunk. One of them might get away and go for help.

But the footsteps were receding. A door opened and closed. The bastards had left them locked in the trunk and Carolyn was relieved.

"Who are you?" Bird croaked. "You were saying something in the van this morning. I can't remember."

"Marilyn Monroe's my sister."

"No joke?"

"No joke. I'm the pretty one."

Bird didn't laugh. "You're not Alton's babe?"

"We're friends." Carolyn wondered.

"I don't have a sister," Bird said quietly. "I don't have a brother neither."

"You've got parents, though? Everyone does."

148

"I did have," Bird said, tossing if off. "So your sister's like a righteous babe in your book?"

"I suppose she's a little spoiled. My parents were older when she came along. I was almost in junior high. She hadn't started grade school by the time I graduated high school."

"Yeah, but you'd stick together, huh? You know, like David and Reno Stouth."

"You think he'll hurt us?"

"No," Bird said much too quickly.

Carolyn tried to roll the kinks out of her neck, stretching it from side to side. She readjusted the folded red leather jacket under her shoulders and scrunched down on the carpeted floor of the trunk.

"You and Rooster aren't married or anything, right?"

"Right," Carolyn said, drawing her knees up.

"I was thinking about marriage. It's not for me. I'm what you call a free spirit. Women, you know, they can't be trusted."

"You're all alike," Carolyn said, clenching her teeth. "I didn't realize you guys turned against us so young." She lay her hands flat on the carpet and pulled her legs up as tightly as she could manage in the small space. She let loose and kicked the trunk lid as hard as she could. The Ford rocked on its springs.

"Hey, cut it out," Bird protested, taken by surprise. "Won't do any good."

Carolyn had bruised the bottom of her feet. They stung. She caught her breath, turned over sideways.

"You know who did it," she said to the fender well on her side of the trunk, "don't you, Bird? You know who killed Dorothy Fleming."

"You could say I have an idea. You don't want to hear about it. If you don't know, it can't get you in trouble."

"It's a little late for that, kiddo."

"Hold on a second," he said. The words came out in small grunts. Bird turned completely over, struggling for purchase on his hands and knees. In a moment, he was straddling Carolyn, groping with his hands, his forehead pressed against her shoulder. She could feel the bristles of his short haircut.

"Hold on, hold on," he whispered as she tried to scoot out from under him. "I'm looking for something."

"I could pretty much tell you where everything is."

"Not that. The tire tool. There's got to be one back here someplace."

"I think I'm lying on it."

"Roll under me then," Bird urged.

Carolyn's fright and anger turned to irrational laughter. She started giggling and couldn't stop. When was the last time a man had said that to her? Bubbles of laughter shook her chest. She was smiling in the darkness.

"Come on," he said. "There's a tire tool, I can pop the lock."

Bird's apartment now looked more like a fourteen-year-old lived there. I ran a quick check of the mess to see if anyone, or any body, had been hidden in the closet, the shower stall. Bird didn't have a car. Carolyn had driven there. They were gone and the van was parked outside. Those were the facts.

Someone had torn into Bird's place. This was a fact. It was clear that neither Bird nor Carolyn had left of their own free will. She would have locked the van. She wouldn't have gone with strangers.

It was the videotape they were after.

But when had the search been conducted? Sammy knew I had the tape. Had someone ripped Bird's apartment to pieces on Sammy's behalf, it had been done before the lawyer and I had conducted our seminar in intimidation in John Wathan's office.

If it were someone else doing the looking, who?

Who could have known Bird had the tape?

Jim.

The condition of Bird's apartment certainly explained what the kid was doing in my van this morning. He was running scared. If he'd used Carolyn as a sacrificial lamb to lead someone on a wild-goose chase, I'd kill him. Or come damn near. No, I'd kill him.

Carolyn knew I had the tape. Back to the facts, I thought. But sometimes the facts aren't enough. You've got to play a hunch. I found Bird's telephone and hit automatic redial. It was a pizza joint that delivered.

I'd gotten my butt off first base, all right. But only to be caught in a pick-off play. I didn't know which way to turn. Which way to run. I was caught in a game and I didn't know the rules. I didn't know all of the players. But I knew the stakes. Dorothy Fleming had lost in an early inning.

I hadn't lost yet. Not by a long shot. I dialed a local number I knew by heart. He answered on the seventh ring.

"Meza?"

"Yeah."

"How would you like to earn a little money babysitting?" I asked.

"Who's this?" he wanted to know. And, "How much?"

There was no tire tool.

Bird did manage to locate an aluminum wing-nut and pried at the latch that held the trunk lid shut. He was propped on one elbow, dripping sweat, cursing quietly. Carolyn was curled fetally at the back of the trunk.

"David Stouth thinks they killed Reno," Carolyn said. "He thinks they killed his brother. They've got my purse, Bird. They know who I am."

"I guess so," he admitted.

He kept working, bloodying a finger, the knuckle of his thumb.

"And I'm the sister. A sister is close enough. A sister is an eye for an eye."

His hand slipped again, scraping his sore knuckle. Bird cursed loudly, lifted his head sharply and banged it against the lid of the trunk. Carolyn wanted to laugh. But she didn't dare. She needed to pee. Laughing might set it off.

"They don't want you," Bird finally said. "Stouth wants whoever did it."

"Bird, it was an accident! Reno couldn't swim. He slipped and hit his head falling into the pool."

"Did you see it happen?"

Carolyn didn't answer.

They heard a door open and close. Footsteps.

Bird stopped clawing at the lock. He'd lost the wing-nut again anyway. Carolyn squeezed her eyes tightly shut.

This time David Stouth had a gun. He stood back, displaying it, expressionless, as his cohort helped unload Bird from the trunk, then Carolyn. Her knees were weak and wobbly. Her dress was ruined. Her hair was matted, damp with sweat. Carolyn couldn't take her eyes from the pudgy revolver David Stouth held as casually as the sky holds rain.

Carolyn stepped toward the big man. She slapped David Stouth on the face as hard as she knew how. He didn't blink. He didn't step back. David Stouth had been expecting it. Nothing could hurt him now that his brother was dead.

He held Carolyn's wrist and stared at her sadly. He didn't want to be doing this to a lady. The four of them walked across the darkened room, toward concrete steps. The door she'd heard open and close was at the top of the steps. Carolyn didn't want to know what was behind it.

"Where's Carolyn?"

"She had a date."

"I thought she was sleeping with you, Dad."

I scowled at my daughter, my left foot on the shiny bumper of Sammy Maxwell's red sports car in M-lot. The game was over. Rowdy was wrong. Gubicza lasted into the eighth and Wathan brought in Tom Gordon, a young right-hander who needed work, to close out the game.

"Well, aren't you going to do anything about it?" Avery held her Royals bag loosely from one hand.

"About what?"

"Carolyn, Da-ahd! She is your main squeeze. I'll bet it's a ballplayer."

"You get any autographs?"

Avery turned luminous, her mouth widening into a large smile.

"Who?" I asked.

"Tell you later if you promise not to detonate."

I saw Marilyn then, striding toward us. The Volvo was nearby.

"It was a shame, wasn't it?" Marilyn asked, her hand shading her eyes in the late-afternoon sunshine.

A shame? The Royals whitewashed the Brewers, 4–zip.

"Rowdy didn't get in," I said, catching on.

"And he's always right about that," Marilyn said as if betrayed. "It's that damn glove. He misses it more than he lets on."

I definitely hoped so.

"Would you mind taking Avery with you? I need to talk to Rowdy."

Avery made a face I hoped Marilyn didn't see.

"Not at all," Marilyn said. "But don't you keep him out too long. You both are invited to sit in tonight when I do my reading. I need all the support I can get."

"Wouldn't miss it," I said. Avery rolled her eyes and, though a fatherly stare of displeasure was called for, I didn't blame her one bit.

"He shouldn't be long," Marilyn continued. "It's not like he'll need a shower. I don't know why they make them suit up if they're not going to play."

Avery turned back to look at me as Marilyn led the way to the Volvo. Her mouth hung open widely and her tongue stuck out one corner as if she were being choked to death. Sometimes you had to smile at the things a thirteen-year-old girl did.

154

I watched a few thousand people trudge toward their cars. Tour buses pulled up and idled loudly while stragglers were waited on. One or two players I recognized found their cars, ignoring pleas for autographs from a group of kids who had massed outside the clubhouse exit.

Sammy waited impatiently while I led Rowdy away from the car, his head bowed to listen, his glasses, I thought, about to pull free from his face and drop. They didn't. To his agent's chagrin, Rowdy shouted back he'd be riding with me. I didn't have an M-lot pass. Hiking to the van on the other side of accompanying Arrowhead Stadium afforded plenty of opportunity for Rowdy to work on his legs.

"You want some money for it?" Rowdy asked as we loped along.

"It wouldn't be right," I said. "The guy who has it wanted to see that you have it back. He probably wants your autograph."

"That glove's been with me since the minors," Rowdy tried to explain. The big left-hander palmed a baseball, working his fingers on the stitches.

"Sorry about you catching fire like that. The bull-pen guys are always playing tricks like that. One time in Texas, I took my cap off out there and they nailed it to the bench. Like to of ripped my arm off grabbing the thing when I got the call to warm up."

He shook his head as if there were no telling what would happen next.

"Nobody knew it was me." At least I guessed they didn't. Avery surely would have said something.

The parking lots were nearly deserted by this time. Rowdy climbed in and complimented me on the van's customizing. Then he talked about RVs and the one he was going to buy. Apparently, it would have its own satellite dish.

Rowdy didn't know Carolyn was missing and I decided he didn't need to know. Sammy Maxwell was the one I'd talk to about that.

I slipped into midtown on Forty-seventh Street.

Rowdy was talking about his wife.

"She's really into it," he said. "And she's sharp, too. Don't let that dumb-blonde smile fool you. But I prefer the stuff that rhymes. You're going to be there, aren't you?"

I wasn't the one who was going to have trouble making it to Marilyn's poetry recital.

I worked my way north, taking the weight off my burned hip from time to time by leaning toward the window.

"Where's this guy live anyway?"

"He's meeting us," I said. "Not far." I crossed on Thirty-ninth, heading for the Kansas state line.

"Maybe I can give him some call tickets for tomorrow's game. ESPN's picking it up and if they don't use me for this one, they may as well send me down. Hey, he's not the guy who stole it?"

"No."

"He's a friend of yours?"

"Let's say I trust him, Rowdy." Rick Meza had already been paid. In Kansas City's underground, you didn't renege on a deal unless you planned to leave town. For good.

Meza's truck was parked just north of the medical center, one block inside the state line. He wanted Rowdy in Kansas and I didn't argue. It was his call. The truck was a '54 black Chevy with an orange Harley-Davidson decal in the rear windshield. I pulled up directly behind it.

"Go with him, he'll give you the glove."

Rowdy had opened his door, then leaned back in to say, "You sure this guy is trustworthy?"

"You can bet on it," I said. "He's just afraid you might be bringing the cops."

Rowdy nodded knowingly. He strolled to the passenger's side of the black pickup, tossing and catching the white baseball in the tan fingers of his left hand. I watched them drive off together, a few pale puffs of oil-enriched exhaust trailing Meza's vintage truck.

Turnabout's fair play in any game. I should have paid Meza to brand Rowdy's rump with a wire coat-hanger. Just enough to make him jump.

As far as Sammy Maxwell was concerned, I reminded myself of the second rule of competition: hold a grudge long enough to get even. If anything happened to Carolyn, I'd pay Rick Meza to kill Rowdy Monroe. Body disposal was one of the biker's known specialties. The way I felt about Carolyn, you could call it love.

Maxwell had lost his star player. I'd lost mine. It seemed to me a trade was in order.

SEVENTEEN

Sammy Maxwell's sports car wasn't in the driveway. The Jeep was, as was Marilyn's Volvo. The Monroe house was the only place Carolyn knew where to get in touch with me. I didn't look forward to spending the night there. The Monroes, I discovered, were fresh out of Boulevard Ale. Jugs of white wine were being chilled in the fridge, for tonight's reading obviously. Two similar bottles of red table wine were parked on the kitchen counter.

I located an orphan bottle of bourbon in one of the cabinets. I hate bourbon, but I managed to choke down the top three inches of this eight-year-old brand. It didn't make sense to me to age something that tastes like pancake syrup.

I couldn't afford to get drunk, but I needed something to put my nerves off edge. My head buzzed and I couldn't sit still. I wanted to act, to do anything, but all I could do to help Carolyn now was wait. Wait for Sammy Maxwell to show for Poetry Hour.

Early May in Kansas City is usually marked by warm

weather and short evenings. Until the days stretched toward August, the nights were cool. I'd stuffed Bird's handgun inside the back of my waistband. To top it off, I'd donned a windbreaker from the back of my van. It was smudged with dust on the elbows and along the collar. I didn't look well-dressed, but I looked about the way I felt.

On the deck were buckets of carryout chicken, disposable plates and utensils, cups of cold mashed potatoes and warm coleslaw. Chicken bones had been dumped in one of the buckets. Three fried wings remained in the other.

"Help yourself, Dad," Avery called. I carried the bucket of too few pieces of chicken to the hot tub. Avery was alone.

I sat on the bench built around the tub, my back to Avery, and munched breaded chicken skin. Normal people know how to eat chicken wings, my mother had always said. I knew enough to pull the bones apart. Anyone who hadn't learned to eat the cheaper pieces of chicken in their youth were too uncommon for my mother's taste, for meaningful conversation. She couldn't relate. And hadn't cared to.

I pocketed my halo. Avery wore a blue Royals T-shirt in the tub, which she'd turned on high, complete with lights.

"It's great, Dad. You ought to try it."

"I appreciate the compromise," I confessed.

"Marilyn gets in naked," Avery informed me. "What a bitch."

Suddenly it seemed I was on the winning team, according to my daughter. Dweeb dad manages to keep head above water, I thought.

"She's not like Carolyn at all," Avery continued, floating in the churning water.

"Marilyn?"

"She's a bitch, Dad. She doesn't listen. She doesn't care about anyone."

"You mean she doesn't care about you. Aren't you being a trifle narrow-minded?"

"She doesn't like you either, Dad, and I don't think she really likes Carolyn."

"Did she tell you about Reno?" I was on my last chicken limb.

"Isn't that *so* radical?" Avery said, holding on to keep from moving with the surges of water.

"Radical," I repeated. That was the word for it.

I tossed in the final bone and set aside the bucket.

"When you get out, I think you'd better pack your bag, Avery. Put your stuff in the van."

"We're not going to drive all night?" she whined.

"I thought I'd get a room at some place really stud," I said.

"Stud?"

"Uh, kickin'?"

"Right, Dad. I'm all for it. What about Carolyn? Are you writing her off 'cause she went out with someone else?"

Avery, the scholar, was sincerely curious concerning the dating ritual of dinosaurs.

"Hardly. I thought you and I would leave after the poetry reading. I'll settle you in, then I'll find Carolyn so she and I can talk."

"You mean I get my own room!" Avery nearly squealed.

"Don't get too excited, dear heart. I'll be in the room next door."

Avery was already clambering out of the tub. She unfurled a towel and rubbed her hair with it. The blue didn't come out.

"Dad?"

"Yes."

"You and Carolyn are sleeping together, aren't you? That's why you want your own room."

"To tell you the truth, Avery, it hasn't come up."

Her face reappeared.

"Maybe if you did, she wouldn't be out with some other guy."

Avery wasn't wearing her cut-offs. I struggled not to mind. She'd waited until she could be in the hot tub alone. She'd waited probably because she was embarrassed to have to wear a T-shirt; still, I was happy with that decision. Avery read my expression and put on her totally exasperated face.

"This shirt comes all the way to here when it's wet, Dad." She pulled the soaked material to below her knees.

"Like I said, I appreciate the compromise."

Avery studied me for a moment. For a moment I was no longer the entirely unreasonable ogre she usually had for a father. What the hell, it was her vacation too.

Bird pounded a metal locker with both hands until Carolyn told him to stop. They were caged inside a small locker room. There were no windows. Bare light bulbs in ceiling fixtures filled the corners with gloom, pushed the darkness against the walls.

Four tiled shower stalls lined a wall. Next to them

161

were two toilets in their stalls. Neither curtains nor doors blocked view of the facilities from the rest of the room. It didn't matter. The light barely reached her knees, crawled up her ankles like spiders.

Carolyn felt diaphanous. If Bird chose to look at her, he would only see the tiled wall behind her.

A long metal bench was the furniture. Metal lockers, one severely dented, lined the remaining walls. Four porcelain lavatories, as large as kitchen sinks and stained, completed the ensemble. In the corner, a metal hamper was overstuffed with used towels and mildew.

One of the lavatories dripped. A wadded pair of jockey shorts had been discarded under another. Carolyn rinsed her hands, but they were someone else's hands. They were practically invisible, nearly useless. They were hands that didn't feel a thing.

She dried the vague, long fingers on her crumpled dress, watching them in the mirror. It was her dress, she knew, but that wasn't her standing there. It was someone else's blue eyes and dark hair, someone else's cheekbones.

Carolyn had disappeared into the shadows. She was back there in a mildewed corner. She'd slipped down the drain in the middle of the sloping concrete floor that had once been painted brick-red. She wasn't here anymore.

I paced the rumpus room. Chairs had been moved in for the meeting. A board had been placed on the pool table and covered by a white cloth. The food, cheese things and crackers, chips, and plastic plates were in position. I helped myself. The videocassette of Dorothy Fleming and Rowdy was tucked under one arm, inside my windbreaker.

A baseball occupied the previously vacant pedestal of Rowdy's trophy shelves. I picked up the smudged ball to see who had signed it. There were only a few signatures on this one and they were all New York Yankees, including Billy Martin. There wasn't anything new about it.

"Your daughter said you would like to see me before the guests arrive."

I replaced the baseball on its wooden holder and turned to look at Marilyn, who stood in front of the couch in front of the fireplace. She wore a red silk blouse like gossip. The folds of silk flirted at the edges, more than hinted at the details of Marilyn's body.

Her eyes were on kind fire, a friendly blaze of curiosity. I wondered what chemicals on this planet would burn with a flame of that color of blue. It was her eyes, not her clothes, that hid the story. It was her eyes that steadfastly refused to reveal anything.

"Sit down," I suggested. "I have something to show you." Reaching inside my windbreaker, I hoisted the videotape with its yellow label punctuated by a red circle.

"No time," Marilyn said. "Perhaps after everyone leaves."

"You have time for this, Marilyn. I think you want to see it."

I didn't imagine it would surprise her. I didn't care. My goal was a reaction, a revelation of any information that might help me find Carolyn.

Walking to the big-screen TV I'd been fooling with while I'd waited, I pushed two buttons and fed in the cassette. The screen lighted with a blur. I had it set on *Pause*.

It was at this point she was supposed to ask me to stop. Still standing, Marilyn refused to give herself away.

"Well, maybe a minute or two, but you must hurry. I really don't have time for all of it."

"I was hoping for a confession," I said.

"A confession of what?"

Screw this, I thought. I pushed the button. The theme to *The Benny Hill Show* filled the room. Lights flickered. I stepped back to look at the screen. I hit fast-forward and watched the late-night reruns speed through a series of slapstick routines.

When I looked up, Marilyn was holding her arm outstretched, offering me her hand and a tolerant smile. "Alton, are you trying to make a pass? I'm nervous enough about tonight. Have you seen Rowdy?"

I accepted her hand. I considered not letting go. I considered twisting it until her face turned blue. I would have beat her senseless with a broom to help Carolyn.

"You're so sweet," she said. "And funny, too. But let's not leave the tape running. My guests will be arriving soon."

Marilyn walked out of the room. I listened to her blouse rustle as she departed. It sounded like derisive, covert laughter. The sound may only have been the swishing of her black skirt trailing pregnant secrets I couldn't make out.

The entire tape was of Benny Hill. I spun it forward and backward. There was nothing funny about it.

The Kansas City poets dressed more or less as normal people. They wore jeans and dirty jogging shoes. Printed T-shirts, button-down shirts. Except for one gray-haired gentleman who was done up in tweeds. Except for Marilyn in her whispering silk.

They acted like normal people, too, gathering in small knots. I had the distinct impression they didn't like one another. Were that the only criterion, it was a group into which I fit rather nicely.

Richard and Gary sat in chairs, looking like kids trapped in Sunday school. Richard almost managed to hide a scowl. Their girlfriends, Sandra and Julie, gabbed away as if they were the only people in the room. Rowdy, we were told, would arrive any minute.

Who was I to argue? When Marilyn gave me our tickets for tomorrow's evening game, I didn't have the heart to tell her that Rowdy might not show. Nor the interest. I was saving this tidbit for Sammy Maxwell, who was himself running late.

The sliding glass doors were open to allow the cigarette smoke to escape. Avery stood in the cool night breeze, seemingly alone, watching the water in the swimming pool as if words were written on the surface.

I stood in front of the weight equipment, which had been moved out of the way, and stared at the Yankee baseball on its little pedestal. I was thinking that I was about to figure out something, but it wouldn't quite come to me.

Reno's death was pretty much as Sammy had restaged it. I tried to place everyone in the house. Carolyn and Avery were upstairs. Marilyn waas upstairs. Rowdy was upstairs. Richard and Sandra and Julie were upstairs. Everyone was changing clothes, taking showers, blow-drying their hair. Or were they?

Sammy had selected Gary to be downstairs for the reenactment. Because he had been downstairs when Reno fell. Sammy had selected Richard to discover the body. Because I had a prison record and an unsavory reputation. Where the hell had Sammy been?

He'd been out in the hall of the ninth floor of the Regal Inn, hurrying from the elevator. The parallels between Dorothy Fleming's murder and Reno Stouth's accident were apparent in Sammy Maxwell's role in cleaning up each mess. It was entirely possible, I realized, he was cleaning up after himself.

I studied the stocky, thick-necked college kid sitting next to Richard. Gary Wright. Sammy Maxwell had pretended not to know his name when he'd gathered the household in the rumpus room. He was distancing himself from the kid. Maxwell had obviously known Gary Wright's name well enough when he and I were having it out in John Wathan's office.

The baseball returned to its stand made sense to me now. That was the easy part. It had been one hell of a pitch that caught Reno Stouth looking, as he was rising from his deck chair perhaps. I pictured Sammy Maxwell handing Gary Wright the ball. I saw Sammy Maxwell sliding open the glass doors. Reno stood, or almost stood. The bodybuilder took a fastball to the head and took a fall.

An invisible umpire called him out. I could hear the splash. I could smell the chlorine. Welcome to the big leagues, kid.

Then I saw what was really there: Avery standing too near the pool with two deep ends.

I joined her. I needed to walk. I needed to run in circles. I needed to do jumping jacks until I threw up.

We stood next to each other and looked at the water. I wanted to tell Avery how fish lived in the sea. They eat each other. But I couldn't think of the words.

"Well, aren't you going to do something about it?" my daughter asked.

"About what?"

"Carolyn, Da-aahd! She is your girlfriend, isn't she?"

"What should I do?"

"Stop moping for one thing."

"Avery, I'm not moping."

"That's what you call it when I do it."

"I'm brooding, considering. Adults don't mope."

"So go find them, Dad. Punch the guy in the nose. Do something to show her how you feel. Carolyn's doing this to make you jealous. You're supposed to stand up for a woman when you're sleeping together."

"We're not going to bed together, Avery. I mean, we slept in the same bed, but we're not . . . uh, you know."

"Sure. And while you're telling lies, what's the difference between brooding and moping?"

"Brooding is when you're thinking about something. Moping is when you're feeling sorry for yourself."

"You're thinking about that muscle guy, aren't you? Me too."

"What about it?"

"I don't think he fell. I think somebody knocked him into the pool."

"Who?" I asked, fascinated.

"Well, I *brooded* on it," she said. "It's that fat one. Richard's friend." She meant Gary Wright.

"Why do you think that?"

167

Avery shrugged. "I don't know, he just looks like it. Richard is good-looking. He's tall."

"What about Rowdy?"

"Are you kidding? He's rich. Rich people don't kill people. They hire someone else to do it. Don't you watch TV?"

"When you were at the game yesterday, Avery, who left?"

"Everyone. They all got in their cars and drove away."

Where did she get such a smart mouth?

"I mean the people here. Who left their seats for the longest times?"

"Mr. Maxwell, I guess. He practically never sat down. He went upstairs a lot, to the suites. He said he was going to introduce me to Coughland, but I guess he forgot."

"Kauffman," I corrected her. "He owns the team."

"So?"

"What about Marilyn?"

"Yeah, she was gone a long time too."

"What about Gary and Richard, and their girlfriends?"

"They were there most of the time," Avery said. "And Carolyn. How many times are you going to ask me who sat where, Dad?"

"That's it," I said.

"You're all done?"

"You look lovely tonight."

Avery beamed. She leaned forward on her toes to whisper something in my ear.

"Everyone knows that was you on the field today," she confided. "But we're not saying anything."

Avery went back in through the sliding glass doors. I

found my way to the kitchen, preferring bourbon to wine. What I still lacked was a line on Jim. Whoever the hell he was.

As if by lightning, I was slugged low in the back as I opened the cabinet where the bourbon had been stored. It was a savage punch to the kidney, taking me totally by surprise. I doubled over with the pain and the force of the attack. Then someone's meaty arm was around my neck, squeezing. I couldn't breathe.

EIGHTEEN

Having your air shut off does something to the sinuses that makes the inside of your head stink. Your ears roar. I hated wrestling.

Finding purchase on the tile floor, I planted my right foot, bent the knee, lowered myself inside the headlock and sprang sharply back and up with my elbow.

It smacked somebody hard. My assailant coughed, loosening his hold. Spinning on my left foot, I brought a right-handed fist around to level someone tall and discovered Gary Wright standing there, a red mark on his chin. My power punch landed on the stocky kid's forehead and I yelped with the crunch of my hand against skull.

Gary pedaled backward, somewhat stunned, reluctant to use his hands, which dangled at his stocky sides. Sportsman that I was, I had more on my mind to getting even than a whack to the forehead. People who attack you need to be taught a lesson so they don't keep doing it. I took out the frustration of Carolyn's absence on the collegian's leg with a vicious left kick meant to fell him.

The chunky kid's backward movement saved his knee-cap and extensive cartilage damage. Still, the leg buckled.

Returning favors, I doubled him into a tight headlock from behind. I saw Sammy Maxwell perched in the door-way, his expression changing from smug pleasure to glum anxiety. I considered ramming Gary Wright's fat head into the countertop. But the grudge was passing. Gary was nothing more than a weighty bundle of gasps for air.

I wanted Sammy to step into the room. Instead, he turned tail and walked away.

I waltzed my heavy load to the kitchen stove, jerked open the oven door with my free hand, kicked loose the baking rack and dropped Gary Wright with a forward shove. He weighed too much to carry around for long.

"You want me to turn it on?" I seethed. I pushed his collapsed bulk farther forward and down with my right foot on his broad lower back. It was the exact spot where I'd taken the kid's initial sucker punch.

Gary seemed to be shaking his head no, his face pinned and bleeding, when I heard Marilyn insist in no uncertain terms that I stop it.

"You're ruining everything," she said bitterly.

I left Gary in his fallen position to contemplate whether Sammy Maxwell had asked too much of him by ordering him to take me from behind. I wrapped a white tea towel around my injured hand and watched Marilyn march back to her affairs of culture. I left the house.

Opening Marilyn's Volvo, I found a half pack of menthol cigarettes and a disposable lighter in a plastic tray that also held pocket change and a dented can of diet soda. Two pieces of skin were missing from my right hand. That was the least of it. Carolyn was out there somewhere and it was killing me.

Out front, I scanned the lawn. It seemed the whole world had Carolyn. The answer I wanted was small, so small it was invisible. A virus you couldn't see, touch, taste or smell. A virus you could only feel when it felled you. It was something small I was after, as small as that distant star. Something so large it snuffed out entire worlds. I closed my eyes to find a name for things evil inside of each of us.

The name was Jim.

I lit one of Marilyn's cigarettes and inhaled. I unwrapped my hand. I stuffed the towel somewhere cozy and, coughing from the menthol, tucked the burning cigarette into the middle of it. My butt itched.

Bird wasn't giving up.

With Carolyn's help, he dragged the long bench to the bolted steel door. They stood the bench on end with some difficulty. Once Carolyn backed out of the way, Bird toppled it onto the brass doorknob. Two more times and the knob popped off.

But the heavy locking mechanism didn't disengage.

The door opened inward, when it opened at all. There was no point in slamming their bodies against it. Bird needed something he could use to pry at the hinges, anything he could insert to trip the bolt mechanism of the lock.

"They could do with a couple windows in this room," he said, dropping on his hands and knees to check out the plumbing under the lavatory basins.

"I wonder if there's anything inside the lockers we

might find useful," Carolyn said. Bird's focused energy on effecting an escape had brought her around.

Bird grunted. He was on his back on the floor, kicking a drain trap loose. The flimsy metal pipe clattered across the room.

"Do you think that will help?" Carolyn sounded unsure.

"No," Bird said, "but we can always flood the place. It'll cost them plenty to have locked us up."

It was a funny idea. But Carolyn couldn't laugh.

I stood in the doorway of the rumpus room. The people seated in the room were an inconvenience of a populated planet. If it weren't for all these poets, I could get down to the business of discovering the identity of Jim. All I had to do was ask the right person in the right way.

Marilyn Sakwoski Monroe stood in her silks in front of the covered pool table, in front of the food, speaking to the gathering in what sounded to me like a drone. The people and the furniture between the two of us merged into a dormant silence, a historical photograph. Sammy Maxwell was there, dapper as usual, avoiding looking at me, avoiding looking at anyone.

"*Your face,*" Marilyn recited. "*My child that swims inside me like a fish, there in the darkness when I lie down . . .*"

Woman as aquarium, I thought. A popular subgenre.

"*I swam with your face between my fingers . . .*"

An explosion interrupted her. It shook the house and the contents of the room, momentarily blasting out all thought. The windows on this side of the house rattled.

"Get in the van," I told Avery, tossing her the keys and

173

pointing to the sliding glass doors. It was an order she couldn't disobey.

I snagged Richard Monroe's arm as he rushed by with the others, behind Sammy Maxwell's mad dash out of the room. He'd flashed by me without a glance.

"This way," I said, ushering him out the back and onto the deck.

"What's going on?"

"Sammy's car caught fire," I told him. "He really should get a gas cap that locks." It had taken the gasoline fumes some time to soak through the tea towel someone had stuffed into the spout. Luckily, Marilyn smoked 100s.

I thought Richard was going to laugh.

"Do you know where the club is?" I asked.

"Club?"

"You know, *Body by Reno*. He and his brother have a health club here in town."

"It's more like a gym."

"Exactly." It had finally dawned on me while I was out front. Jim wasn't a who. Gym was a what. I knew who'd hired Bird to steal the car. And I knew where to look for Carolyn.

"Have you been there, Richard?"

He nodded slowly, still leery, still wanting to be around front of the house.

"Let's go then."

"You want me to go with you?"

"I thought you might want to help find your brother."

"Rowdy? Is he missing?"

Sammy Maxwell's car had been blown onto its side. It was engulfed in flames that smelled mostly of upholstery and burning tires.

Richard wondered aloud who would do a thing like that. It had been meant to stir the hornet's nest, to throw Sammy into a fright. But now I had somewhere else to go. The hornet in question roared out my name and came trotting across the front lawn as Richard and I approached the van. I considered pulling the handgun from inside my belt, from under the windbreaker, but Avery might be watching.

"You did it!" the agent screamed at me.

"Don't jump to conclusions," I barked.

Sammy sputtered. "You took Rowdy," he bellowed. "I saw you drive off with him. You won't leave town a free man!"

Richard stared at the two of us, his mouth open. Avery stared from inside the van, where she sat in the driver's seat, enjoying the show. I hoped she wouldn't tell her mother.

"I'll see to it," Sammy was yelling. He'd worked his way between me and the van. Someone from the crowd was approaching slowly. I could hear her silk.

I pushed Sammy Maxwell with both hands against his shoulders and he sat down immediately in the grass. I motioned for Richard to go around the van and get in. He did. Stepping around Sammy, I noticed his face was a much darker red, caught in the security lights. His eyes refused to blink.

It was all I could do to keep from kicking him in the teeth. Maybe some other time. "See you at the game," I said.

Avery climbed hurriedly into the back. I was blocked in by the students' cars. After two quick pivoting maneuvers, I spun the van up over the curb and across the lawn, sliding past Sammy. I caught Marilyn in the headlights. She stood motionless, looking as if she wanted to go with us. The van rocked on its springs, bounced onto the street after we circled by Sammy's burning car. I heard a fire engine siren.

A black Crown Victoria LX was pulling away from the curb, a half block away. I'd seen it earlier. The two men inside had been watching the house. At first I thought they were henchmen Sammy had hired. Now I knew better. They'd been waiting for the house to clear out.

I stepped on it, but they got a head start on me. Taking a corner at thirty-five, I felt the van tip, heard Avery yelp.

"What's the rush?" Richard said, clutching the dashboard, biting out the words.

I was on their bumper soon enough. The black Ford sedan was driving like nothing had happened. I flashed my lights and they pulled over to the curb. Trusting sorts, I thought, then thought better of it. David Stouth was a man on a mission. Hell, he probably wanted to talk to me.

The driver's window was down. I walked to it.

"Mind if I get in the back?"

A console button popped open the door locks. I climbed inside.

"Where's Rowdy?" the bigger man, the passenger, wanted to know.

"He didn't come home tonight."

"That's not good enough," David Stouth growled. Before we could argue about it, I had my gun against his head.

"Four hands on the dashboard, please," I said. "Rowdy didn't kill your brother."

Stouth started to say something. I told him to shut up.

"I know who's behind it," I said. "I need some time to trip him up."

"Tell me," David Stouth demanded, turning his head sideways.

"Shut up," I repeated. "You've got my girlfriend. I'm on my way to pick her up. Is anyone with her?"

"The kid doublecrossed me," Stouth said, not answering my question.

"Is anyone watching her?"

Stouth didn't answer, except to say that I didn't know where to find her and if I put the gun away maybe we could work something out.

"What I mean is, 'Am I going to kill someone when I get there?' "

"You don't know where she is."

"Who hired you to have Monroe's car stolen?"

"You don't know shit."

The driver was getting nervous. His hands moved.

I couldn't take them with me. It was only a matter of time before one of them did something stupid and my gun went off. The only option I could come up with was to lock them both inside the trunk. So I did. Stouth sputtered a few warnings as I closed the lid.

I found two automatic .45s under each side of the front seat. You have a gun, you should keep it in reach. These would make nice additions to my collection. I popped the hood and removed the rotar cable.

"There's nobody guarding the place," I told Richard as I drove away.

"You sure?"

"Pretty sure."

"Who were those guys? Where are we going?" Avery wanted to know.

"To pick up Carolyn," was all I could think to tell her.

"Was that the guy she went out with?"

"You could say that."

"Why did you put them in the trunk, Dad?"

"Where do I turn?" I asked Richard. "They wanted to be alone," I told Avery. "And please, no more questions for a while."

We eased into town on Truman, six miles an hour over the limit. I needed to avoid being stopped by a traffic cop, but I'd be damned if I was going to drive the posted speed limit.

"You like baseball, Richard?"

"What do you mean?"

"Everybody says you're another Rowdy Monroe." I was fishing.

"That's a laugh. I can barely get it over the plate. I'm no good at it. I don't even know if I want to be."

"How about Gary, a different story, huh?"

"That's the truth. Have you seen him pitch? He lays it right in there, man. Smokin'."

"I figured as much. Has Maxwell already signed him?"

Richard started to say something, then stopped. "I'm not allowed to say anything about that." Not saying anything about it was saying enough.

Marilyn had been wrong in her assessment of Richard's little brother. Rowdy, no doubt, had wanted his little brother to be just like him. And I'd fallen victim to athletic stereotypes. The short, fat kid was an arm to reckon with.

"One thing about Gary," Richard went on, "it's not just power. He's accurate as hell."

"Heat and meat," I said absently, watching street signs.

"Yeah, right." Richard chuckled. "Where'd you pick that up?"

"Cooking class."

I turned a hard right on Troost, through a red light. Sunday night, even the edges of downtown were empty. And so were the streets.

Two blocks west on Eighth, Richard pointed out the place. It was a two-story brick storefront with no outside lights. The first-floor windows had been bricked in. *Stouth Gymnasium* was painted in bright yellow letters where one window had been. Underneath the large, arching letters, a wooden sign had been bolted to the wall. It read, in blue on white, *Body by Reno.*

I didn't need a third sign to tell me we'd found the place. I drove around back. The block sloped off toward the Missouri River. The gym was three floors of brick from the backside. Maybe it's where Rowdy and Marilyn got the idea for their house. The building opened onto the alley by way of a large garage door, two cars wide.

I told Avery to sit up front and lay on the horn if anyone drove up. I told Avery to keep the doors locked. I told her I'd be right back.

"I don't get it, Dad. Are you robbing the place?"

I rummaged through the van, coming up with exactly what we'd need. I handed Richard the bolt cutters out

179

the sliding side-door of the van and jumped out, a steel pig's foot in one hand, a flashlight in the other.

The cutters snapped the padlock in a jiffy. I uncurled the chain, walked to one side of the reinforced aluminum garage door and kicked as hard as I could at the place where the bolt slid into the frame on the inside. Richard stood back and watched, learning new skills.

I kicked the garage door on the opposite side. It made quite a racket, but there wasn't anyone really to hear it. And in this neighborhood anyone who might hear the aluminum door being kicked in wouldn't care.

I lifted my toe under the handle in the middle of the kicked-in door and it clanked smoothly upward as if by remote control. *Voilà!* Another party to crash. Nobody was reading poetry at this one.

If Carolyn was hurt in any way, I knew where to find David Stouth and his cohort.

"You want to drive the van in?" Richard asked.

"No time," I said. "Bring the cutters. They might come in handy."

Richard followed me into the large, dark room. I played the flashlight along the walls and stacked cartons until I located the steps that led to an interior door. Richard had to hurry to keep up.

"I have a gun," I told him. "Anything happens, just lie down flat. I wouldn't want to hurt you."

I fitted the steel curved toes of the pig's foot between the metal door and the jamb. I leveraged it quickly open with a creaking pop, only needing one hand.

"Have you done this before?"

"Quiet," I said. Then, pausing, asked, "Do you hear running water?"

180

There was a makeshift boxing ring in the middle of the room, otherwise littered with outdated and weighty gym equipment. There appeared to be offices at the back of the room and another flight of stairs.

"I guess they don't have alarms," Richard said.

Water poured down the stairs and Richard nearly slipped and fell as we made our way to discover its source. Together, we sloshed toward two steel doors, one with water rushing out from under it. I handed Richard the pig's foot and took out my gun. Something was wrong. There shouldn't be a river here.

Sticking the flashlight in my armpit, I tried the door. The knob came off in my hand. Yellow light shot out the resulting hole as if from a gun. Inside the room, someone was giggling.

"Up yours," Bird shouted. "Hope you got your waders on!" Then he was giggling again.

"Carolyn?" I called loudly. "Are you in there? Where is she, Bird? Carolyn, are you all right?"

Carolyn's laughter joined Bird's high-pitched giggling. The party was on. I used the bolt cutters to bite through the sheet steel around the dead-bolt lock while Richard held the flashlight. Carolyn and Bird gabbed away on the other side of the door. I heard something about being locked in the trunk of a black Ford. A Crown Victoria LX was my educated guess.

"I thought you'd never get here," Carolyn said once I got the door open. She rushed into my arms, the bolt cutters clattering to the floor, making a splash.

"Hey, I thought Rowdy was here," Richard said, staring at Bird.

Bird slipped sideways into the shadows. I quickly put a

stop to that, by encircling him in the beam of the flashlight. "Going anywhere in particular?" I asked. Bird
didn't say another word until we were loading into the
van.

Avery stared at him. He sat down on the seat beside
her, grinning.

"Hey, who's the babe?" Bird wanted to know.

It was the first time I'd seen Avery speechless. She was
either being coy or couldn't think of a thing to say. Either way, a terrifically bad sign that she liked the kid in
the red leather jacket with the strange haircut.

"Touch her with one finger," I told Bird as I climbed
into the driver's seat, "and I break nine."

NINETEEN

Avery camped out in her room at Crown Center. Next door, the team gathered to eat. I didn't know what to do with Richard, but I wanted him present to help put everything together. Carolyn had changed into jeans. Nobody wanted to talk, then everyone wanted to talk at once.

"What did Avery mean about you putting two guys in the trunk of a car?" she asked, her voice overriding my and Richard's false start. She crumpled a fast-food bag and tossed it toward the dresser top from her perch on one of the double beds.

"David Stouth and a buddy of his were staking out the Monroe house. I'd just figured out where you might be and managed to stop them for a little chat."

"That'll teach 'em," Bird said. He sat in one of the upholstered chairs. "Did you hit 'em with anything?"

"They blew up Sammy Maxwell's car." Richard sat on the other bed, sucking a plastic drinking straw, his back against the headboard.

Well, *someone* blew up Sammy Maxwell's sports car, but

who was I to correct a guest? I paced from windows to door and back again. Bird followed me with his head, either curious or afraid of what I might do with my hands when I walked behind him.

"They tore the shit out of my place," Bird bitched.

"Do you think they're still there?" Carolyn asked.

"No. Generally, you can kick out the backseat and get out of the trunk that way," I said. "Sometimes it takes a little while to figure it out."

"They were going to kill us," Carolyn swore. "I think we should call the police."

"We?" I wondered aloud.

"Me, then. I'll call the police. I'll come back for the trial, too, the bastards."

I was shaking my head. "They wanted Rowdy. They were going to trade. David Stouth thinks someone killed Reno. He wanted to get to the bottom of it, to make somebody pay."

"That's not all they wanted," Carolyn said. "What was it they were looking for in your apartment, Bird?"

"The tape," he said off-handedly.

"What tape?" Richard asked, looking from one face to the other.

"First things first," I said to Richard. "Where were you when Reno took his dive?"

"Upstairs. Everyone was upstairs." But his face said, *Well, maybe not everyone.*

I started the list for him. "Rowdy and Marilyn were in their room. Carolyn and Avery were in the guest bedroom. I'd been out front."

"Yeah," Richard said, his eyes bright. "Sandra and Julie were upstairs." He snapped his fingers. "Gary," he added. "Gary didn't come up when we did. He was talking to Sammy in the rumpus room."

"Business?" I asked.

"Maybe," Richard admitted. "Anyway, that makes two. You think Sammy pushed him into the pool?"

"Am I supposed to spend the night here, or what?" Bird interrupted. We ignored him, though I noticed Carolyn smile.

"No, I don't think Sammy did it."

"Gary? Why would he . . . ?"

"Because he could," I said. "And because Sammy Maxwell asked him to. For all I know, he handed him the ball."

"The ball?" Carolyn piped up.

"A baseball from Rowdy's trophy shelf. There was a mark on Reno's temple. It was an easy pitch for someone with the arm and the practice. The sliding glass doors were open. A ninety-mile-an-hour curve would put anyone into the pool at that distance. Reno was a sitting duck."

I didn't tell them about the baseball missing from Rowdy's shelf after the body was found. I didn't mention that someone had put it back later. I didn't have the energy to explain everything and I wanted to use my time to find out some things for myself.

"He could do it, that's for sure," Richard said. "But why? Gary barely knew the guy."

"Like I said, Sammy asked him to. Sammy took care of everything."

"Gawd, Alton, you make him sound like Charles Manson," Carolyn said, shuddering.

"There are similarities. Who hired you to steal the car, Bird?" I asked without looking at the kid.

"What?" he stumbled.

"You heard me."

"David Stouth. I used to hang out at the gym. Sometimes there was some business, you know?"

I understood perfectly. At Harvard they call it networking. "And you were supposed to give him what was in the trunk?"

"Yeah, it was a setup. Hell, the keys were in the car. All I had to do was show up and drive it off. You know the deal, Rooster. I get to turn the car and they get the goodies."

"Only you looked at the tape and decided to hold out."

Bird shrugged as if to say only an idiot wouldn't.

"Why did David Stouth want the tape? How did he know about it?" Carolyn asked.

"It wasn't David. It was Reno. Reno was in the house. Someone told him they wanted what was in the trunk. They confided in him. He said he might be able to do something about it. He made a deal with David, who hired Bird. Only instead of getting paid for the tape, David Stouth ends up with a dead brother and a gut full of revenge."

"You think Sammy hired him through Reno?" Carolyn asked.

It was my turn to shrug.

"Rowdy?"

I didn't answer. Instead, I thought I would let Bird.

"Who did you sell the tape to, kid?"

"I ain't saying anything in front of him."

186

Richard was staring ice at the junior car thief in the red leather jacket.

"It's okay, Bird."

He shook his head.

"I said it's okay! You aren't in charge anymore. You already screwed up enough, don't you think?"

"You don't have to be a shit about it, Rooster."

"Did you sell it to Sammy? I know he was at the Regal."

"No," he confessed.

I'd been wondering. "Well?"

"The babe," he blurted out. "I sold it to her."

"Marilyn?" I asked. Carolyn shot me an evil glance. She started to say that Bird meant Dorothy Fleming, but Bird said, "Yeah. The baseball babe."

All bets were off. "What's in your closet, Bird?" Carolyn wanted to know. "Alton, he wanted to rescue something in an envelope under the carpet in his closet. That's why we went over there. He was afraid—"

"What?" I interrupted, staring at Bird.

"The juice," he said, his dark eyes unblinking. He was afraid to look at Carolyn. He almost said he was sorry.

"Cash?" I asked.

"Postal money order. The dumb bitch filled it out with her name and address and everything. She was supposed to leave it blank. All she left blank was who it was paid to. I had to wait till the car thing cooled down or sell it short, so I stored it."

"How much did she pay you, Bird?"

"Six grand. Look, when I called Fleming she laughed at me. She said she didn't want the tape. So I called the house to see if someone there might want it. I thought I'd get that baseball guy, but the wife answered the phone. I told her what I had and she was real interested."

"And she agreed to pay you at the Regal."

"Why not? I thought after the funny wore off, maybe the Fleming dish would change her mind and I might have a little auction. Hell, she wouldn't even answer her phone. I didn't want to tell you, Rooster, 'cause I figured that blind guy had hired you to get the glove back."

"Which is why Rowdy isn't the one who hired the car stolen," Carolyn said.

"One down, two to go," Richard said, realizing there wasn't good news to be heard in this conversation.

"Sammy Maxwell," Carolyn said definitely.

"No," I said quietly. "If he wanted the tape, he didn't need to have the car stolen. He'd probably seen it a few times himself. Rowdy trusted him with every detail of his life."

"And his money," Richard added.

"Dammit, Alton, no! She's my sister," Carolyn insisted. "Why would she—"

"She wanted the tape without Rowdy knowing she had it."

"It doesn't make sense," Carolyn said, refusing to believe it.

"It does if you're looking at the future from her point of view. That tape could damage Rowdy's career. Sammy knew it. Rowdy would know it soon enough."

"So what! A wife wouldn't hurt her husband's career," Carolyn pleaded, her blue eyes angry with me, angry with the room.

"It's like this, Carolyn," Richard said, rescuing me from saying the words. "She could blackmail him if he wanted, you know, a divorce. If he was going to marry someone else. She could make him either stay or pay dearly to be free from her. Marilyn's hooked on the life, the money, the attention . . ."

I let her think about it. Carolyn kept shaking her head, afraid of the next step her mind would take.

"She didn't kill Dorothy Fleming," Carolyn blurted out. "I don't care what you say. Marilyn's my sister. I know her. She couldn't kill anybody. Alton!"

The room was so quiet you could hear the traffic seven floors below on Pershing Road, even with the windows closed.

"Why Reno?" Richard asked, still not satisfied.

"He knew everything," I explained. "He was the go-between. He talked to your brother. He talked to Marilyn. He set it up. When everything went to shit, thanks to Robin Hood here, Reno became a threat to Rowdy's career."

"You mean to Sammy's career, don't you?" Richard corrected me.

"Exactly."

"You going to give them Gary?" Bird was the only one in the room besides myself who was considering what would happen next. "David Stouth isn't calling it quits."

"Stouth thinks Rowdy had something to do with it. Anyway, he seems to want Rowdy badly."

"So give him Rowdy. Hey, Rooster, let *them* work it out." It was uncanny. It was almost as if the kid knew I could hand Rowdy over to David Stouth and company. I wouldn't have dreamed of it. I had someone else in mind.

"Call him, Alton," Carolyn said, insistent. "Call Rowdy and tell him everything. Then I talk to Marilyn.

Get this out in the open. You know that little bastard in the business suit killed Dorothy. You know it!"

"I saw him at the Regal, Bird," I said, turning on the kid so I wouldn't have to look at Carolyn piercing me with her eyes. Looks can't kill. But they can hurt like hell at times. "Did you?"

"Yeah, sure. But he didn't see me. The whole ballpark came over, I thought. That's why I got out of there, Rooster. I didn't want him following me to your van. I didn't want to get you in trouble."

"That settles it," Carolyn said. "Do you hear me? That settles it. Sammy Maxwell killed Dorothy Fleming. I don't care how and I don't care why. He did it."

But he hadn't killed Reno Stouth. That seemed important to me. His role in Reno's death was pronounced, but it wasn't Sammy who'd pulled the trigger on that fastball. He'd been careful about that.

"Did Gary leave the game, Carolyn? Think back."

She looked at Richard.

"They left together," she finally said.

"We went upstairs," Richard said, not realizing he was suspect. "We were meeting people in the suites, the booths. He was with me the whole time."

"If I'm spending the night here, I ain't sleeping with no guys," Bird interrupted.

"Sammy and Marilyn both left the game long enough to get out of the parking lot, cross the street, show up at the Regal and get back," I summarized. "Unless there's an ex-boyfriend of Dorothy's in the picture, it's between the two of them."

"No, it isn't," Carolyn sputtered.

She looked at Bird, her lips quivering. Something kept

Carolyn from saying it out loud. Whether she wanted to say it or not, it was clear she considered Bird a suspect. The only question I had was why she was so reluctant to point the finger at him.

"Look, I can get my own room," Bird said.

"You'll stay here," I told him. I almost told him not to whine. Being a father was becoming a habit of mine. "We'll get a rollaway. Avery and Carolyn get the other room."

"Maybe I should go home," Richard suggested. It was obvious he didn't want to. I couldn't blame him.

"You'll end up in the middle of it, if you do. Sammy sees you come in, he'll tie you to a chair and stick a lamp socket on your toe to get you to tell him what we've been doing. Of course you can swim, can't you, Richard?"

Bird chuckled.

"Yeah, I guess you're right. It won't help Rowdy if I'm there."

I would have made him stay, sleeping on the floor in front of the door with my gun on my belly, if he hadn't agreed it was a good idea. Richard not only knew too much for his good, he knew way too much for mine. And Carolyn's. And, for that matter, Avery's. Besides, Rowdy wouldn't be coming home tonight.

One nice thing about murder in the family, nobody wants to call the cops. Of course, Bird and I didn't consider the authorities a viable option. The cops gleefully put the little guys in jail when they have trouble catching the big ones. Ask around.

TWENTY

Bird crashed on the rollaway. He'd had a long day. After laughing at my last pair of birthday boxer shorts, the energy drained out of him and he nearly fell asleep sitting up with his eyes open.

Richard and I occupied the beds. We left the drapes closed. Richard wanted to talk.

"You think he showed her the tape?" he asked.

"Who?"

"Rowdy. You think he showed it to Marilyn?"

"No."

"I don't either. My brother's an asshole, but . . . How did she know about the video?"

"She could have found it any time Rowdy was out of town with the team. All she had to do was open the trunk."

"My brother isn't a good husband," Richard continued in a soft voice, "but he was trying, you should know that. Rowdy had broken it off with Dorothy when Marilyn turned up pregnant. That's what caused everything. Dorothy came back after him. He was in love with her.

192

He was in love with both of them. But he wants the kid, you know. He really wants a kid. My brother's an asshole, but you've got to understand he was trying to fix things."

"Do you think Marilyn killed her?" I asked.

"It makes sense, doesn't it?" Richard replied. There was nothing for me to say. My butt was itching and my knuckles stung. I couldn't go to sleep. I couldn't get the picture of Dorothy Fleming's surprised look out of my mind.

Reno's demise was insidious. I could see Sammy Maxwell handing Gary the ball, sliding open the glass doors. I could see Reno rising from the deck chair. The windup. The throw. I could also see Sammy Maxwell standing in the kitchen doorway when the little bullmoose from Wichita State suckerpunched me.

I saw Sammy Maxwell's car sideways in the driveway. I saw his car on fire. Maybe I'd done it out of spite. I'd wanted to break him loose, drive him over the edge. I wanted him to attack me, to spill truth in rage from his liar's mouth. It wasn't my fault that the explosion had blasted something else loose, that the answer to the puzzle of "Jim" exploded inside of me in a white flash. No more than it was my fault the creep had a full tank of gas in his car.

Something about red silk, something about red sports cars. They were team captains, Marilyn and Sammy Maxwell. They even dressed alike. I saw her standing bewildered in the yard, caught like a rabbit in the headlights, caught looking. I couldn't make sense of her poem. I held up my hand in the darkness, looking at my spread fingers. What was the line? *I swam with your face between my fingers*. Her face was there now, between my fingers. I slowly made a fist. I wouldn't call it swimming.

I must have fallen asleep. Someone was pounding on the door. Richard was sitting up in bed, afraid to move.

With Bird's .32 out from under my pillow, I got to my feet. There are guns that can kill you through locked doors if you let the person on the other side know you're standing there.

"What?" I yelled, standing back.

"Alton!" Carolyn's cry came through weakly. "It's me."

Through the peephole I could see she was alone. I could see she was crying.

Letting her in, I flipped on the lights. Bird was gone. But it didn't matter at the moment. Carolyn rushed inside and I closed the door behind her.

"I've been calling all night, Alton. No one answers the phone. Something's wrong. I can feel it."

"Calm down," I tried.

"Alton, she's my sister! You've got to help. Those men . . . Sammy . . . somebody could have . . . could have hurt her."

"It's all right," I said. "It's all right." How much sleep did a guy need anyway?

The black Crown Victoria LX was in the driveway. The trunk was open. It looked like they had broken the lock. Sammy's burnt sports car lay on its side, coated with white powder, something the fire department had used to put out the fire. Gary Wright's Jeep was gone.

From the front no lights could be seen inside the house.

"We can go around back," Richard suggested.

I drove on by, hoping no one saw the van from one of the darkened windows.

"We can help each other over the fence, get in that way," he said.

Good enough.

Circling behind the Monroe house meant about four blocks of driving, including a quick turnaround in a cul-de-sac. Recent history told me that if anything bad had happened in the house, all we would find was a body. Or two.

Still, it never hurt to be prepared. I found a roll of silver duct tape in the back for each of us. And I handed Richard a loaded gun, one of the heavy .45s from David Stouth's car.

"Wear it inside your shirt until we cross the lawn. These people see a guy cutting across the yard with a gun in his hand and all hell will break out."

"How do I shoot it?"

"Try not to," I said, showing him how to take the safety off. We chambered a round. "Shoot over their heads. Shoot at the sky if you have to. The idea is to keep someone from coming after you. Hide behind something and shoot high, but only if there's trouble."

We wore the rolls of tape on our wrists.

I wanted to say something about guns not caring who they killed, but there wasn't time for all that. Mostly, I didn't want Rowdy's little brother shooting me by accident.

There were trees on this side of the block and they came in handy. One after the other, we darted from one tree to the next, moving quietly, stopping at each tree to

195

catch our breaths. The popsicle fence was a snap to get over. I went first and had Richard hand the gun up before catching hold of the top and pulling himself over.

We landed in a far corner of the yard, the pool between us and the house. Upstairs lights burned in a rear window. We moved in a crouch, our shadows growing short under the security lights, then disappearing altogether until they showed up behind us, growing long.

I sat down in the grass at the edge of the deck, my back against the planking. Richard followed suit, breathless.

"We have to go around front now," I told him. "If someone's here, we want him coming out the front door. We can't do shit out here."

"We could go inside," Richard suggested, his eyes wide from adrenaline.

"Not on your life."

We made it to a corner of the house, where I told Richard what I had in mind. He was to be positioned to the side of the front door, just off the stoop.

"Hit him with the handle of the gun," I told the big kid. "Hard. Aim for the side, for his ear. You understand?"

He nodded, frightened.

"Just don't shoot the damn thing, okay? And make sure the safety's on."

Keeping close to the house, ducking under windows, I made my way to the garage doors at the head of the driveway. I crawled toward the Ford, rolled over on my back and slid under the hood. Opening the door of the Ford would risk being seen from a window when the dome light came on. I didn't need to pop the hood to do my little job, but it wasn't easy finding the wires in the darkness under the car.

I jerked one free and, by feeling, tied the bare copper strands to the accompanying wire. A ceaseless blaring of the horn was my reward. I pushed myself out and made it to the garage doors, stood up, flattened against the doors.

It wouldn't be long. I edged back toward the front door of the house. But the big door pulled open and the storm door swung out before I could get near.

"Who's there?" David Stouth's buddy called. He stepped off the stoop. He didn't see me. He was looking at the car, then scanning the reaches of the lawn. Richard sprang forward from behind, wielding the heavy handgun in a wide arc.

The .45 went off upon contact with skull. There was a bright flash of red and yellow. The shot sounded as loud as a bomb, ringing down the street, waking dogs who'd managed to sleep through the sounding of the horn.

"Ka-rap!" Richard yelled. The gun jerked from his hand, jumped to the ground. He'd forgotten to put on the safety and I was afraid it would go off again. He danced from one foot to the other as the man who'd come out the door crumpled in front of him.

"Get back," I called to him, hoping he hadn't shot his hand. I was on one knee, my gun in both hands, my elbows propped on my leg. I had it aimed at the door. I didn't want to shoot David Stouth. But I would have if he pointed a gun at me.

Richard saw me. He dropped to all fours in the grass. He retrieved the gun and dog-crawled back to the wall of the house. We waited like that for what seemed like forever, no thanks to the blaring horn. I was appreciative of big yards, however. No one had yet shown up from next door.

And no one stirred inside the house. No one came to the door. No one turned on a light you could see from out front.

"Are you okay?" I finally asked in a hushed voice.

"Yeah," Richard drawled dejectedly.

"Stay put," I said. I hurried to the Ford, dropped to the driveway, reached under the grillwork blindly and jerked the wires. The horn died.

"Is he out?" Richard asked when I returned.

"You can count on it," I assured him. "We better wrap him up, but I don't think he'll be home from dreamland for a few hours."

Wrap him up we did. By the time we were through, David Stouth's comrade looked like a silver-tape cocoon.

"Around back," I said, not trusting the front door now. Nobody had said David Stouth was an idiot. He could be standing in the foyer, waiting comfortably to blow away whoever opened the door.

I found the gun David's pal had been carrying, a snub .38. You had to wonder where these guys got all the guns. One more and I'd be able to open a pawnshop. I half-expected to find a machine gun on a tripod in the rumpus room.

"You think Rowdy's home?" Richard asked as I slipped open the sliding glass doors from the deck. No, I certainly didn't. A breath of air washed out of the house. We went inside, guns held straight up by our faces like TV cops do.

TWENTY-ONE

The digital clock in the master bedroom blinked 2:03 in red numerals. Marilyn Monroe was bound and gagged in a laced-top negligee, probably satin. This was the night for distressed damsels. I should have business cards printed up.

Marilyn was on her stomach, mostly, her wrists and ankles tied with white cord. A length of rope, pulling up her legs from the knees, joined her bound wrists behind her back. Everything looked taut. Marilyn's face was red. Her eyes bulged. A wide strap of tape covered her mouth.

I carry a little something in my pocket that will cut just about anything. I'd never in my life learned to untie a knot. I cut her free in moments. Deep red ruts marked her wrists and ankles.

Marilyn didn't say thank you when we eased the tape from her mouth and she choked out a wadded rag meant to hold her tongue in place.

"That bastard," she spat. "He isn't coming home tonight."

If Marilyn meant Rowdy, she was right about that. What was left of Marilyn's mascara were dark smears crossing her cheeks. Her emotions seemed to play the range between anger, terror and, then, disgust.

"Those chickenshits took off," she blurted out, rubbing her wrists, sitting up. She shook back her hair from her face, straightening her neck, lifting her breasts against the lace. I tried not to notice. "Dirty bastards! They wouldn't even tell me where they were going. Didn't ask me to come along. Shitheads. I'm going to kill Sammy Maxwell and those punks. Rowdy's going to fire his pansy ass the minute he gets back, the lousy son of a bitch."

I guess that made me about the last decent guy left on the planet. Until Richard showed up from his check of the other rooms on this level. He sucked the torn skin between his thumb and forefinger, where the action of the .45 had caught his flesh when the gun went off.

He looked from Marilyn to me, then decided to look elsewhere.

"How many were there, Marilyn, who tied you up?" I asked.

Marilyn stared at me for a moment, trying to decide who I was, it seemed.

"Two," she said bitterly. "David Stouth and his bozo. Stouth took off. He's waiting for a phone call when Rowdy gets here and that son of a bitch ain't showing up. I told them that. It sure the hell isn't the first time."

She sounded as if she might cry now, trembling as if from the cold.

"Richard, make some coffee." I looked at Marilyn, who

didn't look like she wanted to get up. "Would you like something to drink? I have to be going soon."

Richard left. He missed the waterworks. Marilyn blubbered into her hands and there wasn't a thing for me to do.

"It's all right now," I said.

"Hunky-dory," she spat, catching her breath. "What the fuck do you know?"

"I know you have the videotape," I said icily. "I know you paid to have Rowdy's car stolen."

She stared at me, gaping, her face wet. Then her reddened blue eyes focused elsewhere. "I thought having a baby would be enough. You'd think it would be enough. You think I'm looking forward to getting fat, to pissing my panties every time I sit down or stand up! Oh God, I don't want to look like that."

Marilyn wasn't crying now. She was thinking.

"They tortured me, dammit. They wanted Rowdy and they tortured *me!* I told them he wasn't coming home tonight. They wouldn't listen."

We'd been through this. "I know you were at the Regal when Dorothy Fleming was shot."

She pinned me with a hard stare. "You don't know shit, cowboy. You don't know shit." With that, Marilyn spun herself to the edge of the bed and vomited on the plush carpeting. It smelled as bad as I felt. She got to her feet and stumbled into the adjoining bathroom, groaning, muttering curses.

"I'll be downstairs," I called through the open door of the john. Marilyn was on her knees by the tub, running water full force from the tap. I didn't care if she heard me. I'd seen horses broken down in the homestretch that

201

had to be shot that looked in better shape than Marilyn, but there wasn't an ounce of me that wanted to help her.

I didn't have anything to prove. I'm not a police officer. I'm not an officer of the court. And I'm not even sure I believe in justice. Truth's another matter. I needed to know who had killed Dorothy Fleming. And, if I could, I needed to know they wouldn't get away with it. But that wasn't up to me. With any luck at all, it would be presented for a jury to decide.

Somebody else needed to gather evidence. All I needed was to know. And not beyond a reasonable doubt. I needed to know for certain. I mentally flipped a coin. It came up Marilyn as often as it came up Sammy Maxwell. Not good enough.

I couldn't present evidence on Bird's behalf, but I believed the kid. She was dead when he got there.

As for Reno's death, I'd tell David Stouth one way or the other. If I had a brother, I'd want to know if some punk pitcher capped him. That some punk lawyer on the usual money and power lust trip set it up and took care of the mess afterward. Of course, it would be better if all this were printed on the front page of the morning newspaper.

Richard and I stood in the kitchen, watching coffee drip into the pot.

"The car's not here, he won't come back," I said, talking about David Stouth.

Richard sucked his wound, the torn flesh between thumb and forefinger. Would it keep him from throwing a forkball? Did he care?

"Who'll tow it this time of night?"

I rubbed my thumb against my own fingers in a gesture that meant money talked.

"Call any of the twenty-four-hour services, tell them ten minutes is two hundred bucks. Tell them fifteen minutes is a hundred. They'll get the idea. But wait till I'm out of here."

"You're not leaving me alone?" Marilyn said from behind us. "You can't."

"Richard's here," I said, turning to look at her. A different woman entered the kitchen in bare feet and a terry-cloth robe.

"Don't worry, Marilyn," he said. "I've got a gun." He picked it up from the counter next to the coffee maker, using the wrong hand. It wasn't confidence-inspiring to see him dangle the .45 upside down.

Marilyn's hair was wet and she'd washed her face. Without makeup she was prettier than Carolyn. Something to do with the way her lips were shaped. Her eyes were wide and blue and frightened. She looked helpless. I knew better.

She motioned me out of the kitchen, freezing Richard into place with steely eyes. I trailed Marilyn into her sitting room, feeling like a puppy caught taking a dump on the Oriental rug. Marilyn found her cigarettes and lit up. Her hands were shaking. The red marks on her wrists looked like bracelets and I wondered how she might look in a pair of handcuffs.

"It's not safe here," she said. "You can't just go. Rowdy's not coming home. He does this all the time."

If she pleaded with her eyes, I wasn't watching it. I picked up the phone, my back to her, and dialed Crown

Center. Carolyn picked up. "Everything's fine," I said. "I really can't talk. I've a little errand to run and I'll be right there."

"That bitch," Marilyn seethed even before I could disconnect. "She's has a hold over you, Alton. What is it, blowjobs? Or does she take it in the butt?"

The whole world had turned against Marilyn, including her sister. And she was fighting back the way she knew how. Name-calling. I wasn't going to discuss it.

Marilyn dropped her cigarette into the ashtray and opened her robe. She smiled like the devil. "Well, darling, I can do that." She put her hand on her crotch, something she picked up from watching baseball. The rest of it she must have learned on her own.

"And I can do it all night," Marilyn added. Once would have been plenty. I knew better than to argue with a woman when her hair was wet, so I simply turned and walked.

"No!" she screeched.

"He'll be at the game," I said, stopping to face her head-on. I could handle this. At least from a distance I could. More than a roll with Marilyn, I wanted a drag from her burning cigarette. "See you there."

"The bastard'll be at the game. Oh, you can count on that! But if I were you, I wouldn't be showing up."

Marilyn had closed her robe. Her trump card had failed to take the trick. But it wasn't her last card.

"I ain't mad at nobody," I said.

"Sammy's setting your ass on fire," she said, coming up with one person I was mad at. As for a burning butt, I'd already been through that. "He's setting you up."

204

I shrugged.

"You're going back to jail, Alton. What will Avery think about that?"

"And you can help? Don't tell me you're my guardian angel. With angels like you, sweetie, I guess I'll just go straight to hell instead."

I could have used the coffee. I drove the van across the Monroe lawn, which was beginning to look like a demolition derby arena. Richard and I rolled David Stouth's cocooned pal to the side of the van and managed to get him up and inside the sliding side-door. He groaned in his sleep.

"Get in the damn Volvo," I said. "And go somewhere. Take her anywhere, Richard. Spend the night in another county."

He was shaking his head. "She won't leave," he said. "Rowdy could walk in the door anytime, you know? He could come home now or at dawn."

"Well, good luck." He was going to need it. Richard held up the gun and grinned. He might need that too. No telling what Marilyn might do.

I dropped off our would-be butterfly at a shelter for the homeless in the River Quay district. If he didn't wake up by morning, someone would do the honors. I propped him against the brick wall next to the door. It was a lot of work, but he'd be safer out of the street.

And so would I. I don't know when shift-change was supposed to take place. David Stouth would show up at the Monroe home sooner or later. When he saw the car gone, he wouldn't go in. He might even call it a day and get some real sleep.

Besides, it was Rowdy he was after. And Rowdy wouldn't be coming home this morning, no matter what Richard thought.

TWENTY-TWO

It wasn't despair. And I probably wasn't disconsolate. It's just that the real world and the people in it had managed once again to piss me off. I was trying not to be disappointed with mankind, but, you know what? I prefer horses. They run their hearts out and they either win or they don't. So I lose a few bets. Nothing a horse does can fill me with disgust.

And these were "nice" people, to boot. An American sports hero and his beautiful wife. Relatives, for crying out loud! Carolyn's sister and brother-in-law. You couldn't figure people. I wouldn't put two bucks down on one of them.

I needed sleep.

"I'm ready when you are," Carolyn said, turning me from the floor-to-ceiling window of my room at Crown Center. I'd been trying to see what Rowdy could see over the fence in his backyard.

The expression on my face, in the glow of the television set with the sound turned off, must have given me away.

207

"I'm ready to leave when you are, Alton. I don't like it here."

"We can go from the game. We'll hit the highway from the ballpark."

"Do we have to go to the stadium?"

"I do," Alton said.

"Why?"

I couldn't tell her everything. "Bird's showing up," I said. "He's bringing the money order—" I'd started to say *with her name on it.*

I turned my right hand over and flexed my fingers. The broken skin over my knuckles tore. It was part of the healing process.

"I'm sorry I got you involved in all this," she said. "I just thought it would be a nice trip." She tried to laugh. "I just wanted to get away from the rain." Carolyn closed her eyes, leaned her head back on the headboard.

I sat down on the bed next to her and patted her leg.

"Everything's gone wrong, Alton. I don't even like my sister anymore. I feel sorry for her. I want her to snap out of it . . . Oh Alton, do you think she did it?"

Carolyn's eyes were open now, blue and wondering. "Do you think Marilyn killed that woman?"

I didn't answer.

"It could have been Sammy," she said.

"Shhh . . . We'll know tomorrow or we'll never know."

Carolyn needed to hug somebody and I guess it was me.

"Everything's gone wrong but you, Alton," she said, her chin on my shoulder. She tightened her hug, holding

208

on, and I tightened right back. We both needed something strong to cling to. We had each other.

"They're not happy," Carolyn said. I felt a tear against my neck. I felt her eyelash. "That's the worst part. Marilyn's miserable and she likes it."

We didn't want to let go. We didn't want to look at each other.

"What about you, Carolyn? Are you happy?"

She pulled away finally, studying my face. My hand found its way into her hair. Her mouth was parted and, before either of us could think of a good reason not to, we kissed. Her mouth was warm. We couldn't stop. We fell back on the bed together, pressing against each other, holding. Nobody laughed.

We made love gently and deeply, silently.

When I came to, I was alone. It was early morning, a soft gray light filling the windows. I heard the shower. Carolyn would be leaving soon, sneaking back into her room before Avery woke, which was generally about noon.

I had a choice to make. I could play dead and let her walk. We could pretend it hadn't happened, which might be what Carolyn preferred. We could go on the way we had been. We could talk about it on the phone once we were back in Louisville. We could say to each other that it would never happen again.

She would say, "Can you believe how stupid we were?"

And what would I say? Nothing, probably.

I had a choice to make. I pulled back the plastic curtain and stepped into the shower with Carolyn. I couldn't stop smiling. There were things I wanted to see with the lights on. And one of them was Carolyn's eyes smiling back at me in a situation just like this.

It was fun this time. We nearly fell, giggling, nibbling, testing our sea legs.

"You know what?" Carolyn said, facing me, standing back, the warm shower soaking her.

I shook my head.

"That tattoo of a fighting cock isn't so bad, but I always wanted to see this other one." She was cradling me in one hand. Who was I to argue with a woman when her hair was wet? I supposed we'd both had our fantasies. Mail this to Cooperstown, I thought. We were going for an inside-the-park home run.

You like the idea of dying broke, give a thirteen-year-old your credit card and free rein in the Crown Center shops. Among the souvenirs she bought were an automatic camera, ten rolls of 35mm film, three swimsuits, a leather skirt, designer hosiery, earrings, two pairs of shoes, a pair of red cowboy boots . . . and a shirt for me. It was an extra-large Hawaiian affair with black-and-white spotted cows in place of flowers against a field of blinding yellow.

I'd been sleepy when she and Carolyn left to visit the mall of fancy shops built onto the Crown Center Hotel. I was waking up now. The cows reminded me of some horses I'd bet on over the years. The shirt came to my knees.

"Happy birthday, Dad," Avery said as I buttoned on the bovine beauty. She held the camera to her face and it flashed twice. "I knew you didn't like the shorts, but this is really kickin'."

"Living large," I said. The shirt would make nice curtains if I ever bought a turquoise mobile home.

"Well," she said, screwing up her face. "It looked better in the store. Maybe if you did something really cool with your hair."

After the fashion show, Avery crammed her swimsuits into her Royals bag. I asked to see her autographed baseballs, thinking I hadn't paid enough attention to my daughter. They were all signed by the same player.

"Stan Mahoney? Who's that?"

"Stan Mahaffey, Dad! He's this really rad usher. He had a ponytail and his ear pierced twice."

We all have our heroes. "Run next door and get ready," I said. "I have a phone call to make."

"Sure you don't want to take another shower while I'm gone?" Avery flashed the camera at me again.

"What is that supposed to mean?"

"Gawd, Da-ahd! They could hear you in the lobby. Was I supposed to sleep through that?"

"Avery!"

"Well," she protested, "the showers are back-to-back."

"Not another word, Avery. And not a word to your mother, either. About anything, young lady."

"You mean you and Carolyn? I already told her all about that. You've been doing it for, like, forever."

"Avery, we have not. But your mother doesn't need to know about any of this."

"Oh, like the guys in the car last night that you pointed a gun at?"

"Exactly."

"The dead guy in the swimming pool, Dad?"

"Yes. You know, Avery, I've been thinking. Maybe we

didn't come to Kansas City at all this weekend and maybe you get to keep all this stuff you bought?"

"You can count on me, Dad."

"And all these pictures you're taking, why don't I get them developed for you? I'll put them in an album and keep it at my place."

"Sure. Besides, you must think I'm a real geek. If I said anything she wouldn't let me have any fun again. I like staying over at your place."

"You do?"

"Yeah, it makes me feel like I'm grown up. Mom won't even let me drink coffee. Says it's not, you know, good for my health."

What the hell's wrong with coffee? I wondered, dialing Rick Meza's number. The biker let his phone ring, as usual, a dozen times before picking up.

"It's Rooster. How's the boy?"

"Hung over. Guy ain't used to tequila and ludes, what can I tell you?"

"That you'll drop him off at the ballpark—in about an hour."

"Yeah, sure. Thanks for the business."

"And Meza?"

"Yeah."

"Give him the glove, all right?"

Rowdy Monroe would be late for the team meeting, but there was little I could do about that. I've never been a stickler for rules. And this way, David Stouth couldn't meet up with him until after the game. I'd have the answer I needed by then. I'd be on the road to Louisville with the two loves of my life.

Carolyn had been right. There was someone I could call from a pay phone in St. Louis. Someone in Kansas City who would write down the details of the story I told him concerning Reno's death. Someone who would understand when I refused to identify myself. Someone who would send round a black-and-white to pick up Sammy Maxwell for questioning. Someone who'd have Gary Wright brought up from Wichita to the big leagues, on a murder rap.

Carolyn wore a new summer dress and, to my surprise, a touch of lipstick. Avery took our picture in front of the indoor waterfall in the lobby of Crown Center. Carolyn and I stood with our arms around each other and found it comfortable to walk like that.

Bird was late for the game. I'd given him my fourth ticket. He'd know where to find us when he got there. I counted on the little punk not to bail out.

The nationally televised Monday night game was another early-season sellout. The starting time had been moved up an hour to allow for network scheduling. The Royals were batting by the time we found our way inside the stadium. Richard and Marilyn sat in front of a number of empty seats, behind the home-team dugout.

Gary, along with the college girls, was back in Wichita by now. Sammy Maxwell could have been anywhere. Marilyn wore dark sunglasses and didn't turn around to look at me as I plopped down in my cattle shirt in an empty seat behind her. Carolyn slid in next to Richard. Avery took the aisle seat, but mostly she was somewhere else, taking flash snapshots of some totally radical young man in the concession lines, no doubt.

I was caught up in the game. It was a pitcher's duel. Zip-to-zip. When Jackson finally connected in the fifth, I spilled beer in my lap in my rush to stand and shout nonsense at the top of my lungs. There's truth in a home run you can't find elsewhere. When it goes over the fence, there's nothing for lawyers to argue about, nothing to distort.

Bo's solo homer landed cleanly—a white dot carried by the roar of the fans—in the real grass behind and above the left-field fence. They'd measure this one.

Agents and million-dollar contracts caught the crowd looking. It was something the owners and the players didn't want you to see. When the fountains came on above the right-field fence, I was thinking they came on to wash the dirt away.

Truth was what agents had taken from baseball. Truth was their lousy ten percent. Maybe in a hundred years, I'd get over it. Right after I began, finally, to understand love.

TWENTY-THREE

From my seat I could see the Regal Inn across I-70. I tried to pick out the window of Room 931 to one side or the other of the Royals' twelve-story scoreboard. Dorothy Fleming watched from the window to see if I could even the score.

Then I turned back to the game. These were great seats. I watched the expressions on the faces of the players as they anticipated a batter's swing. I heard the catcalls from the dugout and attempted to lip-read what George Brett was jawing about on first base.

Baseball is a subtle, sexy, primitive sport. Men picked up sticks to fend off stones. Baseball is the practical science of rocks being hurled to fell a foe. Every man on deck looked to me like a lumbering mastodon waiting to be made extinct. One wooden tusk, instead of two ivory ones. They chewed tobacco like cuds of grass and fell into the pit, the batter's box, swinging their one long tooth at a round white stone coming like lethal harm right at them.

Baseball was Ice Age stuff. And so was murder, I figured.

I focused off toward the bull pen between batters. It seemed miles away, isolated from the game, a habitat occupied by the offspring of alien life-forms, millionaires and madmen caged to protect the mainstream. Rowdy Monroe was warming up.

But even from seats this close to the action, you could only tell it was Rowdy by the number on his shirt and the fact he threw left-handed. Two outs, two on, they called him in. The crowd was pleased and said so. His ERA flashed on the scoreboard.

I watched him trot toward the huddle of manager, catcher, and starting pitcher on the mound. The lights glinted off his glasses once he took the field. And it came to me just like that. I knew who'd killed Dorothy Fleming.

I no longer needed Bird to show up with the money order Marilyn had filled out. I'd meant to show it to her, to have her take her sunglasses off, to watch her expression. Surely I would have been able to see murder in her blue eyes if murder lived there. It was as good a plan as any. Bird had agreed to help me out.

Rowdy's warm-up tosses to Bob Boone behind home plate looked off. But that was his trademark. Randall Monroe's glasses seemed to be pointed right at me. He used only three pitches to test the mound. Each was high and hard.

Boone sprang to his feet and tossed the ball to Kevin Seitzer on third, who sailed it to Brett, Frank White on second, and Kurt Stillwell between second and third. The infield played back. They didn't need a double play and when Rowdy was hit he was usually hit long. Jackson, Eisenrich, Tartabull crept in to catch one on the fly.

The Brewer at the plate only swung once on three straight strikes. Heat and meat, Rowdy was cooking. I pretended I knew what that was like. After all, I'd been on the field during a game.

The kids ran out to drag the dirt around the bags while the fans stood in unison to sing "Take Me Out to the Ball Game." The seventh-inning stretch arrived and, like everyone else who didn't want to miss any of the game, I headed for the rest rooms, edging past the beer man in the aisle who'd made my row a regular stop on his route.

A kid with short dark hair, wearing a red leather jacket, was leaning against the tunnel wall as I approached.

"About time," Bird bitched. "I thought you were going to sit there the whole damn game."

"You were late," I said.

"No kidding."

"Come on down and watch the close," I said. "You bring the money order?"

"Sure I did. That was the deal, right?"

"Go ahead and cash it," I said. "We don't need it now." Bird followed me to the men's room.

"Go ahead and cash it?" he was saying. "That's the thanks I get?"

Bird stood next to me at the trough.

"She did it, Rooster. We have to nail her ass or they're going to nail ours, don't you get it?"

I was busy taking a leak.

"She did it, then she came downstairs to meet me. Sammy sees her in the lobby, he goes up after she leaves.

217

After her car drives off. You go upstairs and he's on his way back, 'cause of course I got away, and he takes the babe's stuff to make it look like a robbery."

"That's it, huh?" I said, zipping up.

"Yeah, see, if Sammy done it, what the hell is he going back up there for? He'd have stolen her stuff the first time around. He's not that dumb. He's a prick, all right, but he ain't stupid."

We were washing our hands.

"We got to nail her, Rooster. You bring a gun?"

I shook my head. "You?"

"Someone else has mine, you know what I mean," Bird said, rolling his eyes. "I thought that was why you were wearing that stupid shirt. You could hide a tank in there. What are those things anyway, cows?"

"Hurry up," I said, leaving. "I don't want to miss the eighth." No telling when I'd ever have seats this good again.

Bird trailed behind me. "You're going to watch the game, Rooster? You're going to sit there and watch the friggin' game?"

I stopped. "Yes, I am. Then I'm going to get in my van and drive home. It's a few hundred miles east of here."

It sunk in. Bird looked as if he might cry. "You're leaving me dry? You're going to dog me, just like that, Rooster? Shit man, I'm taking a walk. I'm getting out of here."

Bird spun on his heel and was gone, breaking into a run as he rounded the concession stands and disappeared. That's when I saw Sammy Maxwell.

He stood in the short, wide tunnel between the seats and the concession stands. He pointed at me with his left hand. His right hand was stuffed into his jacket pocket and I knew what that meant. It meant Bird was right and I shouldn't have left the .32 in the van. The red-faced man had a few good reasons of his own to feel desperate about things.

"We have to talk," Sammy said when I'd walked up. I could see our seats from here. Avery was mysteriously back in hers. Marilyn, Richard and Carolyn were similarly accounted for. All I had to do was keep Sammy away from the seats.

"Listen to me, Franklin. I can take care of everything. Forget about the car. I've got this thing in a tight wrap. Everybody goes home free."

I wasn't afraid of him. Even with a gun in his pocket, Sammy Maxwell wasn't a man to do his own dirty work. He'd proven that often enough already. He was saying something about my coming with him.

Two steps away, I leaned in, bumped from the rear by a fan carrying a cardboard tray of beers back to the field-box seats.

The way for Sammy to have saved his star client was to have Dorothy Fleming dead.

"He did it, didn't he?" I said, staying in striking distance in case Sammy decided to turn toward the dugout seats.

"Let's talk," Sammy urged, moving away, jerking his head.

"He traded uniforms and walked out of the bull pen," I said loudly. It didn't matter who heard. "Or someone wore his number out there in the first place." I stuck a hand hard against his shoulder, pinning him to the wall.

"The players covered for him. He went to see her,

Sammy. He went to see her early in the game. And you drove him!"

"I didn't want to," the red-faced man stammered. "It was stupid. I tried to stop him . . ."

I slapped him, confident he was too much of a chicken-shit to use the gun in front of all these people. I slapped him hard.

"No, you didn't," I seethed. "You didn't try to stop him, Sammy. You handed him the gun! You told him it was the only way. You told him to do it, just like you told Gary to fastball Reno into the pool. You told them you would take care of everything."

No one seemed to be listening, though fans leaving and returning to their seats gave Sammy Maxwell and me plenty of room. Sammy's hand had gone to his face to cover the sting of my assault.

"Did you want to get me in the parking lot? Is that it, Sammy? You got the fat kid, Gary, out there in my van? You going to hand him the gun?"

I doubled back my fist this time, but Sammy saw it coming. He ducked fast, bent forward, and butted me in the stomach, pushing for freedom. His hand-tooled leather-soled shoes clicked on the concrete as he rounded the concession stands.

I hate running. It's what horses are supposed to do. But a man responsible for two murders was getting away from me. He was getting away from everyone, taking his crummy ten percent with him.

The rat-faced little prick had convinced Randall Monroe the best way to start his new family was to shoot Dorothy Fleming. I pictured the two of them standing over her in Room 931. Sammy handing Rowdy the gun.

There'd been no signs of a struggle. Dorothy Fleming must have thought they were putting her on.

During the seventh-inning stretch, or any time really, Rowdy walked back to the bull pen dressed as a batboy or one of the ground's crew. He put his jersey back on, while Sammy returned to Room 931 to make it look like a robbery.

There were two murderers in the ballpark. One had just taken the mound in the top of the eighth. The other was on the run. My cow shirt flapping, I was right behind him, without the slightest idea what to do if I caught him other than beat his brains in until the ballpark security made me stop.

I didn't know it at the time, but a third murderer was trailing us both. A stocky kid with a bad haircut.

I pushed through the lines at the concession stands, running the circular route behind Sammy Maxwell, who was already dashing up the concrete ramp that turned in wide spirals before opening up on View Level, the high seats in Royals Stadium.

Even though I'd quit smoking, I was out of breath and nearly lost the little man as he darted down Aisle 312. Turning the sharp corner, I caught sight of a uniformed officer and pointed wildly toward the place where Sammy had gone.

The officer lifted his walkie-talkie and was saying something about the situation, as I huffed by without pausing. Sammy had run all the way down the aisle steps to the rail, was stepping sideways in front of seated fans, making his way to another aisle to effect his getaway.

I made a wild dash down the concrete steps. The seats were a sea of protesting faces as I shoved between the first row of seats and the rail. I hadn't the breath to apologize as I toppled cups of beer, snagged purses, flattened nachos and banged ankles.

Rowdy threw his first pitch of the inning when I caught up with Sammy, who'd finally met his roadblock, a large man in a white T-shirt. He looked like someone had shaved a bear and stuck a Royals cap on his head. I pushed around him somehow and grabbed Sammy by the shoulders of his jacket at the bottom of Aisle 310. We stood against the rail.

Gary Wright appeared at the top of the aisle, a baseball in his hand. Sammy Maxwell struggled to remove the gun from his pocket. The batter swung. I caught Sammy's chin with a vicious uppercut, still holding his suit shoulder in my left hand. Gary went into his windup.

Maybe you saw this on TV. Robin Yount popped up out of bounds, high above the field-box seats behind home plate. Gary came down on his left foot and released the ball just as a kid in a red leather jacket crashed into the stocky collegiate pitcher at the knees and they went rolling down the concrete steps of Aisle 310. The pitch had been released. Surrounding fans were on their feet, shouting.

Sammy Maxwell collapsed against the rail. I was still holding him with one hand when Gary's fastball hit high and slightly to the right of the middle of my back, killing an innocent cow. Bob Boone, mask discarded, stood at the edge of the backscreen behind home plate and, along with the center-field camera, had the best view of me and Sammy going over the rail just above the press boxes.

We brought the entire stadium to its feet. Forty thousand people gasped in unison. Free-falling, I tried to disentangle myself from Sammy.

My life didn't flash before my eyes. Neither did thousands of faces. What I saw were quick glimpses of the TV announcers we passed, the bull pen, the fountains, the scoreboard, I-70, the Regal Inn, the fountains again. I smelled someone's breath. It may have been my own.

I swear the air caught in my too-big shirt, slowed the fall, even though Sammy and I slammed into the screen over the seats behind home plate together.

It felt nothing like a trampoline. It felt like Sammy's knee had punctured my lung. We rolled, my ankle trapped and held back momentarily by one of the cables supporting the screen. Then I saw Bob Boone's face. The catcher's mouth was a black O, his mitt held up in front of him to snag what was supposed to be a pop foul ball rolling lazily over the edge of the screen.

Rowdy had come in toward home plate. Hitting the screen had felt like hitting pavement. Tumbling onto the turf felt like more of the same. Sammy hit first. I screamed silently with the sharp pain of a broken ankle as I landed on top of him. I'd had the wind knocked out of me when Sammy's knee had cracked two ribs on our first bounce. It was a hell of a ballet.

Sammy's gun landed a foot away. Bob Boone, athlete that he was, was backing up rapidly, banging into the home-plate umpire who had his arms up to call time-out. My lungs screamed for air. My back hurt. I passed out and came to almost instantaneously.

I wanted to tell someone to cut off my ankle and please hurry up about it. But I couldn't speak. I couldn't move except to writhe lamely. Sammy was out cold.

But Rowdy was still in the game.

The left-hander blinked through his thick lenses and slowly understood what must have taken place. Sammy Maxwell was caught, which meant he was caught too.

A teenage girl with a stripe of blue hair climbed over the fence at the end of the dugout and scrambled toward home plate in red cowboy boots. If I weren't dead, she'd kill her father the dweeb for doing this to her. Both teams were ambling out of the dugout. I made it as far toward standing as I could manage: on my hands and knees, retching for air. I looked like a dog who'd been hit by a truck. I looked like a yellow pasture of dead cows.

Through blurred vision, I watched Rowdy scoop up the gun in his left hand. Through the loud ringing in my ears, I heard Avery say, "Dad, are you all right?"

I wanted to say I was fine, to say that a murderer had just picked up the gun. Pitching forward on my knees, I tried to point with a flailing arm. Uniformed security guards streamed onto the field, off-duty cops with licensed guns.

"I've been waiting for someone to do that on a pop-up," one of the players said to another one.

Maybe you saw this on TV, when the guard and the players turned from the fallen bodies and formed a semi-circle of gaping faces. When the off-duty cops unholstered their guns and six-foot-four "Blind Boy" Rowdy Monroe, wildman left-handed pitcher for the Kansas City Royals, had nowhere to run, so backed up steadily with his young hostage in his right arm, a .32 automatic against the blue stripe of hair that stuck straight up like a feather.

Still unable to take air, I turned onto my side. Then

turned over again. I saw the thousands of fans on their feet. I heard their boos like nausea wash over me. The bull-pen gates had opened, the relievers frozen in place as they realized the ace closer had a girl and a gun.

Rowdy was behind second base, backing toward the center-field utility door beneath the Royals scoreboard. I believed I could see her face from here. Avery was terrified but she wasn't crying. A breath finally came and I managed to scream, "No!" It came out a strangled whisper. By the time I got to my feet, hobbling a step forward on my crippled ankle, Carolyn was beside me, holding me up. Other fans poured onto the field but stood in milling groups just in front of the seats.

"She'll be all right," Carolyn said. She was lying. Or maybe it was a prayer.

And maybe you saw this on TV, Bob Boone chucking the ball to third. Seitzer relaying the throw to left. A couple warm-up tosses. Rowdy in deep center field was getting away. Maybe you saw what has become known on sports pages as *The Throw:* Bo Jackson letting one go with the force of a line drive.

Maybe you saw the pitcher collapse, one lens of his Coke-bottle glasses shattered. Maybe you saw exactly where the ball struck home. Or maybe, like me, you only saw the young girl released from a baseball-gloved grip as the pitcher tumbled onto the center-field turf. Saw her run toward the infield, shrieking, Frank White catching her in his arms and trying to calm her. Give the man another Golden Glove.

I couldn't bring myself to watch the television replays on the network news. I didn't want to remember it. I loved my daughter too much to be proud of what I'd put her through, to boast of the team autographs on my plaster casts.

Maybe you saw it all on TV. Or maybe you saw the picture of Avery with a gun to her head on the cover of *Sports Illustrated* less than a week later. Avery's mother did.

Caught Looking is Randy Russell's third Rooster Franklin mystery. He is also the author of *Blind Spot* and the Edgar-nominated *Hot Wire*. His fourth mystery, *Doll Eyes*, also featuring Rooster Franklin, will be published later this year. Randy Russell lives in Kansas City.